Tw
One

Don't miss a story in Harlequin Bla...
12-book continuity series, featuring irresistible soldiers from all branches of the armed forces.

*Heat up your holidays with A Few Good **Marines...***

DEVIL IN DRESS BLUES
by Karen Foley
October 2011

MODEL MARINE
by Candace Havens
November 2011

RED-HOT SANTA
by Tori Carrington
December 2011

Uniformly Hot!—
The Few. The Proud. The Sexy as Hell!

Available wherever Harlequin books are sold.

Dear Reader,

When I was younger, I briefly worked as a reporter for a daily newspaper, but dreamed of becoming an investigative journalist. However, I soon discovered that getting into people's faces when they were at their most vulnerable wasn't something I was very good at.

When journalist Sara Sinclair stumbles across a salacious story that could catapult her own fledgling career into the limelight, it requires her to get into the face of one seriously badass marine who is *anything* but vulnerable. But somebody will stop at nothing to prevent her story from being publicized, and she must depend on Sergeant Rafe Delgado to keep her safe, or risk losing everything...including her heart.

I love writing sexy stories about military heroes and the women who can't help but fall in love with them. I hope you enjoy Sara and Rafe's story!

Happy reading!

Karen Foley

Karen Foley

DEVIL IN DRESS BLUES

TORONTO NEW YORK LONDON
AMSTERDAM PARIS SYDNEY HAMBURG
STOCKHOLM ATHENS TOKYO MILAN MADRID
PRAGUE WARSAW BUDAPEST AUCKLAND

Recycling programs
for this product may
not exist in your area.

ISBN-13: 978-0-373-79644-1

DEVIL IN DRESS BLUES

This edition published by arrangement with Harlequin Books S.A.

For questions and comments about the quality of this book please contact us at Customer_eCare@Harlequin.ca.

www.Harlequin.com

Printed in U.S.A.

ABOUT THE AUTHOR

Karen Foley admits to being an incurable romantic. When she's not working for the Department of Defense, she loves writing sexy stories about military heroes and heroines. Karen lives in New England with her husband, two daughters and a houseful of pets. She loves to hear from her readers, and you can visit her at www.karenefoley.com.

Books by Karen Foley

HARLEQUIN BLAZE

353—FLYBOY
422—OVERNIGHT SENSATION
451—ABLE-BODIED
504—HOLD ON TO THE NIGHTS
549—BORN ON THE 4TH OF JULY
"Packing Heat"
563—HOT-BLOODED
596—HEAT OF THE MOMENT

For my girls, who want to write.

1

Nothing good ever happens after midnight.

At least, that's what her mother always said, and Sara Sinclair was inclined to believe her. Glancing at the digital clock on the dashboard, she saw it was just twenty minutes before that fateful hour. And for the last few miles, she'd been following a sports car along a dark stretch of country road, keeping a safe distance as it careened crazily from one side of the road to the other, narrowly missing the guardrails. She had no trouble believing the driver was drunk, but the amorous attentions of his female passenger were probably more to blame for his erratic driving—Sara watched as the woman's head bobbed over the driver's lap, popping up briefly before disappearing again below the dashboard.

She gave a snort of disgust, and reached for her cell phone to call the local police. The driver was fortunate that he hadn't caused an accident on the winding road. At any other time, she might have found the love-birds amusing, but not tonight. All she wanted was to get home, strip out of the confining evening gown she wore, and curl up with a warm blanket and a mug of hot chocolate. A mere six hours ago, she'd been vibrating with suppressed excitement at the prospect of attending the annual Charity Works Dream Ball, a $750-per-plate black-tie dinner to raise money for injured marines. But now that it was over, she felt empty and disappointed. Not with the event, but with herself.

Someday, she'd learn to be more assertive and speak her mind, instead of worrying about what others might think. She chanted the mantra silently: *Be more assertive.*

The glittering charity ball was one of the most-attended social events of the autumn season in Washington, D.C. Sara had been thrilled when her senior editor had invited her to go, especially since she was only a junior contributor on the writing staff of *American Man* magazine. She spent hours debating what to wear, fantasizing about what adventures the evening might hold. But try as she might, she couldn't figure out why *she* had been selected to attend the prestigious event, rather than one of the senior writers. Even when the guest of honor had stood up to speak, she hadn't clued in.

Marine Corps Gunnery Sergeant Rafe Delgado had been dazzling in his formal dress blues, and Sara hadn't been the only woman in the ballroom unable to tear her gaze away from his broad shoulders and sinfully handsome face. The man was simply stunning, and his voice could only be described as intoxicating, like dark, smooth whiskey…

"That's the guy I want you to interview," her editor whispered in her ear. "I'll introduce you after the speeches are over. Delgado is a bona fide hero, and I'm counting on you to get an exclusive interview with him for the magazine."

Sara turned to her editor with disbelieving eyes. "Because he supports a charity that benefits his Marine Corps brothers?" She arched an eyebrow. "It's noble, but I wouldn't call it heroic."

American Man magazine featured stories about prominent and powerful men across the country, and while Sara had interviewed men from all walks of life, she'd never been asked to do a story on a guy simply because he'd supported a good cause. Not unless he'd backed that good cause with millions of his own hard-earned dollars, and Sara was pretty sure that kind of contribution was way above a gunnery sergeant's pay grade.

The older woman gave Sara a tolerant look. "For someone who claims to be a journalist, you're remarkably uninformed. Sergeant Delgado is the marine responsible for rescuing the three American aid workers in Pakistan."

Sara couldn't prevent a small gasp of astonishment. "That was *him?*"

Lauren Black gave a small shrug of concession. "Well, him and his team. But Delgado was the mastermind. Don't let his pretty face and fancy dress blues fool you. From what I hear, that guy is one tough son of a bitch. Smart, too. He speaks about a dozen different languages."

Sara stared hard at the other woman. "How do you know this? None of the news reports ever identified who the soldiers were."

Lauren smiled and gave her a conspiratorial wink. "Let's just say I have reliable sources in very high places."

Slowly, Sara turned her attention back to the man in dress blues. This was the special-ops soldier responsible for carrying out the spectacular rescue of the aid workers? She recalled the incident from the previous month, when the workers had been taken hostage by Taliban forces. Like so many others, she had been riveted by the story of their dramatic rescue. But through it all, the five men credited with the brave act had never been identified. Two of the soldiers had been seriously injured during the rescue operation, yet they had still managed to bring the three women to safety.

After the speeches were over and the dancing had begun, Lauren expertly steered Sara through the crowds until they reached Sergeant Delgado's side. Engaged in conversation with a group of tuxedoed men, he didn't immediately notice the two women. Sara took the opportunity to get a good look at him, and something fisted low in her abdomen as she studied his chiseled profile.

He'd been gorgeous from a distance, but she hadn't been prepared for the raw masculinity the man exuded up close. On a scale of one to ten, Sergeant Delgado was a ten to the tenth power. He was taller than she'd realized, and the cut of his dress uniform did little to hide the powerful musculature of his body. If anything, the short navy jacket and gold cummerbund only drew attention to his flat stomach and lean hips.

Sara was contemplating the neat fit of his trousers across his delectable backside when he laughed, and the deep sound caused delicious pinpricks of sensation to rise up on her skin. Her heart began to thump heavily in her chest in anticipation of actually meeting him, of having his attention focused on her. She must have made a noise, because all the tuxedoed men looked at her questioningly.

Then Sergeant Delgado turned toward her, and Sara went a little weak beneath the full force of his scrutiny. His black eyes drifted slowly and deliberately down the length of her body, and she didn't miss the heated interest that had flared in their depths.

"Lauren, it's good to see you." One of the men reached out to take her editor's hand. "Lauren is a senior editor with *American Man* magazine," he explained to the group.

"And this is Sara Sinclair, one of my best feature writers," Lauren gushed, pulling a reluctant Sara forward. "Her stories are garnering excellent reviews."

As Sara watched, Rafe Delgado's expression grew shuttered and remote before he flicked his gaze over her one last time. Sara had the sudden sense that she'd been scanned in much the way a laser beam would read a barcode. He'd examined her, identified her and dismissed her. The only indication that she'd made any impression at all was a tightening of the muscles in his lean jaw.

It took all of Sara's self-control not to inspect herself for physical flaws. She knew she looked good. Better than good, actually. She'd borrowed a cobalt-blue Carolina Herrera gown from a friend and had styled her hair in a loose, elegant up-do. She'd kept her jewelry to a minimum, opting for a pair of glittering faux-diamond earrings and a matching bracelet around one wrist, and had taken extra care with her makeup—but the way Sergeant Delgado looked at her, she might as well have been wearing burlap. A part of her wanted to turn and walk away, not only because she suddenly felt gauche, but because she knew instinctively in that moment that he would refuse to give her an interview.

Then Lauren Black worked her magic, talking with knowledge and enthusiasm about the Semper Fi Fund and the way it was changing the lives of injured marines and their families. Sara watched Sergeant Delgado's eyes sharpen on the editor, but when Lauren asked if he would consent to an interview for *American Man* magazine, he inclined his dark head in assent.

"Fine," he said curtly.

"Thank you," Sara replied. She extended her hand to him, but he either didn't see the gesture, or deliberately chose to ignore it. After an awkward second, she dropped her hand and curled her fingers into the fabric of her skirt. For a brief instant, their gazes clashed and Sara floundered in the depths of his dark eyes. Flustered, her breath caught when he shifted his attention downward and focused on her mouth, and she was unable to prevent the warm rush of heat through her veins.

He broke the contact first, withdrawing a card from his wallet and handing it to her. "I'm on leave beginning tomorrow. Call me and we can work out a time."

And then he all but turned his back on her. Sara stood mute with dismay at his rude dismissal of her, but before she could find the words to tell him that she had no interest in writing a story about him, Lauren had dragged her away.

"We did it," she crowed once they were out of earshot. "This will be the pièce de résistance for the December issue! Make sure you call him first thing tomorrow to arrange the interview. Don't give him a chance to forget who you are or what he agreed to do."

Sara barely contained an indelicate snort. She was completely certain that Rafe Delgado never forgot anything and there was no way she'd call him in the morning. He'd probably expect her do so, and a perverse impulse made her want to do the opposite. Besides which, she wasn't exactly looking forward to the interview, not when they'd tricked him into agreeing to it in the first place.

"He thinks we're interested in doing a story about his charity work with the Semper Fi Fund," she hissed to Lauren. "How is it going to look when I begin asking about the hostage rescue, especially when he's never publicly acknowledged his involvement?"

Lauren popped the olive from her martini into her mouth and winked at Sara. "Why do you think I selected you?" she asked, chewing on the garnish. "Have you looked in the mirror lately? You could pass as Nicole Kidman's younger, sexier sister. He'll be so busy thinking about your amazing cleavage, he won't care what you ask him. Just make sure you wear something that puts those girls on display."

Sara blinked and looked away to hide her confusion. Had she really been invited to the ball because of her breasts? Had Lauren been lying when she'd made the comment about Sara being one of her best feature writers?

From the time she had been twelve years old and an investigative journalist had paid a visit to her elementary school, Sara had wanted to be a reporter. She had been fascinated by the stories that the woman, a White House correspondent, had told, and had imagined herself in the nation's capitol, uncovering scandals at the highest levels. She'd never wavered in her dream and had majored in journalism before pursuing career opportunities in Washington, D.C. Unfortunately, despite her success as a journalism student, she hadn't been able to break into coveted publications such as the *Washington Post*. Instead, she'd been offered the position as a junior writer for *American Man* magazine. Now she wondered if she'd only been hired because of her looks. She turned back to her editor, determined to say something.

Seeing her expression, Lauren made a dismissive gesture. "Oh, pish. Don't look so offended. You have great boobs, and don't think he didn't notice. And anyway, this is Washington—information leaks occur every day. He'll just think you're an astute journalist to have made the connection between him and the hostage rescue. Why else would you want to talk to him?"

Um, maybe because he was one of the hottest guys Sara had ever seen? Maybe because any woman in the room would give her left arm to be alone with him? Sara bit her tongue, but decided to make her escape from the ball as soon as she could. The magic of the evening was lost, somehow, upon discovering she'd only been invited on account of her breasts. Okay, that wasn't strictly true. The sparkle had dulled when Sergeant Delgado had looked right through her. Not that she'd expected him to fall at her feet—but to look at her as if she'd been invisible? In that regard, Lauren had been wrong; he hadn't noticed her *or* her breasts. Why hadn't she called him out on his rudeness? Or made a clever rejoinder? Why had she been silent?

And why did she even care?

She didn't know the first thing about the guy. For all she knew, he could be married with kids, but somehow she didn't think that was the case. A guy like Sergeant Delgado was married to the marines. Which was a shame, really, considering he had the most compelling eyes she'd ever seen and a body to die for….

Sara gasped, dropped her cell phone, and stomped hard on the brake pedal as the car in front of her veered sharply across the road and over an embankment and then slammed head-on into a tree with a sickening crunch. She came to a halt, her heart slamming hard in her chest. There was no movement from inside the other vehicle, although the interior lights were on. Steam hissed out from beneath the hood in soft, swirling plumes.

Glancing in her rearview mirror, she saw that the road behind her was dark and silent. They hadn't passed another car in almost ten miles. Unbuckling her seat belt, Sara groped blindly on the floor of the car for her dropped cell phone, swearing softly when she failed to locate it. Sitting up, she looked at the mangled car and drew in a deep breath. She'd find the phone later; right now she needed to find out just how bad the accident was and if there were any injuries.

Flicking her hazard lights on, she climbed out of the car, lifting her long skirts carefully above her ankles as she picked her way over the embankment toward the vehicle. What if they were both dead? Or worse? She wasn't squeamish by nature, but recalling what the couple had been doing in the seconds before the crash, she had no wish to see if the driver had been…dismembered, so to speak.

Biting her lip in fear of what she might find, Sara approached the passenger's side and cautiously peered through the window. Both the driver and passenger airbags had deployed, and beneath the billowing fabric, Sara saw both occupants scrambling to adjust their clothing. She turned away to afford them some privacy, hugging her arms around herself in the chill autumn air. When the driver's door opened, she turned around gratefully.

"I'm sorry," she began, "I just wanted to make sure you were okay. Are you hurt or..."

Her voice trailed off in shock as she recognized the silver-haired man who stood pushing his shirt into the waistband of his pants, bleeding from a cut over one eye and looking both aggravated and shaken. What in the world was Edwin Zachary, senior advisor to the President of the United States, doing out here at this late hour?

Suddenly, Sara wished that she hadn't stopped, that she didn't have to witness this event, because without even looking inside the car, she knew his female companion couldn't possibly be his wife. Diane Zachary was one of Washington's most beloved women, a philanthropist and generous patron of the arts, and a renowned hostess to diplomats from around the world. Sara couldn't imagine her doing anything improper, never mind going down on her husband while driving.

As if to confirm her thoughts, the passenger door of the car swung open and a young woman practically fell out, laughing a little as she struggled to her feet, pushing her long, dark hair out of her face. She wore a miniscule strapless dress that barely covered her breasts, and based on the creases and wrinkles across the front, Sara was certain that just minutes earlier, the silky fabric had been shoved down around her waist. Definitely not Diane Zachary.

"I told you to keep your hands on the wheel," she

admonished, her words slightly slurred. "That was the agreement. Ohmigod, Eddie, you're *bleeding*."

"Colette." Edwin's voice was tight and controlled as he gave the woman a meaningful look. He turned his attention to Sara. "Thank you for stopping, Miss…?"

"Sinclair," Sara replied automatically. Her voice sounded small. "You *are* bleeding."

He touched the area with his fingers, grimacing as they came away smudged with blood. "It's nothing. A scratch." His voice was brusque as he reached into his jacket pocket and withdrew a slim, leather wallet. "I wonder if I could impose on you to do me a favor, Miss Sinclair? I don't want to keep this young lady waiting in the cold until a tow truck arrives. Would you mind driving her home? I'll compensate you for your time and gas, of course." Pulling out several bills, he extended them toward Sara. "And I'd appreciate it if you didn't mention this…incident…to anyone. Higher insurance rates and all that—I'm sure you understand." He gestured for her to take the money.

Appalled, Sara took a step back, raising her hands to indicate she had no intention of accepting the cash. "No, that's not necessary, really." She glanced at the other woman, who swayed unsteadily on her feet. "I'm happy to drive your friend home, but I can't accept your money."

Colette picked her way with exaggerated care across the grass and draped her arms around Edwin's neck. Her dress barely covered her curvy rear end. Reaching out, she plucked the bills from his hand. "I'll take care of this for you, Eddie. After all, I think I've earned it."

Edwin relinquished the money without argument. "It's, uh, getting cold and my On-Star alert will have notified emergency responders of the accident." He disentangled himself from Colette's grasp. "You should get going."

"We're leaving," Colette assured him, tucking the money into the small purse that dangled over one shoulder. Stretching upward, she pressed a kiss against his jaw. "I hope we see each other again soon."

Sara turned away, uncomfortable. "I'll wait for you in my car."

Through the windshield, she watched as Colette walked unsteadily over the embankment toward her. Edwin Zachary had pulled a cell phone out of his pocket and was holding it over his head, trying to find a signal.

"Well, this is awkward," Colette said as she climbed into the car and shook her hair back. She gave Sara a sidelong look, taking in her evening gown and jewelry. "You look like Cinderella running from the ball. Where's your Prince Charming?"

Sara smiled, surprising herself. She thought of Sergeant Rafe Delgado, who certainly had looked like a prince, but couldn't be called charming by any stretch of the imagination. The Prince of Darkness was more like it. She shivered as she recalled the way his black eyes had swept over her.

"There is no Prince Charming," she replied lightly. "Where am I driving you to?"

The address that Collette gave her wouldn't put Sara too far out of her way. Glancing at the digital clock on the dash, Sara guessed she could drop the other woman off and still be home by midnight. Cinderella, indeed.

They drove for several miles without speaking. Sara cast a furtive glance at Colette, who was humming softly beneath her breath. This had to be the strangest night of her life. "So...you're friends with Edwin Zachary, huh?"

Colette shot her a sharp glance. "You know him?"

Sara focused on the dark road and tried to keep her voice neutral. "Well, no, I don't *know* him. But I recognized him—he's one of the president's senior advisors."

There was a brief silence. "Would you believe me if I told you he's my uncle?"

Sara gave the woman a tolerant look. "Uh...no."

"Really, I can explain—"

"Please," Sara interrupted, putting up a hand. "You're both adults. What you do is none of my business. I'm not sure I really want to know, anyway."

"Turn left here," Colette said, indicating a side street that led into a neighborhood of brick apartment buildings. "You can let me off at the next building."

When Sara pulled up to the curb, Colette reached for the door handle and then paused. "Listen," she said, turning to Sarah, "you seem like a nice person. I know this looks bad, but it's not really a big deal. Men will be men, you know?"

"Sure." Sara nodded in agreement, just wanting the woman out of her car so she could go home. She forced a smile. "Have a good night."

Colette sighed, and then pushed the door open. "Thanks for the ride." As she tried to climb out of the car, the long strap on her purse caught on the emergency brake between the seats. With a small noise of frustration, Colette gave it a sharp yank, but the purse snapped open and spilled its contents across the seat. Colette swore softly.

"Here, let me help you," Sara said, and leaned over to

scoop money and cosmetics back into the pocketbook before handing it to the other woman.

"Thanks," Colette murmured, still leaning into the car. Her eyes met Sara's across the seat. Her voice was low and urgent. "Listen…about tonight… Forget what you saw, okay? Go home to whatever upscale little community you come from and go on living your fairy-tale life." She glanced at her watch. "But you'd better hurry, Cinderella. It's after midnight."

2

SARA WOKE UP THE NEXT MORNING with gritty eyes and a nagging headache. She'd spent a restless night, the events of the evening replaying themselves over and over again in her head. And when she did finally fall into a restless sleep, sometime around 3:00 a.m., her dreams had been filled with disturbing images of a darkly handsome man, his body moving over hers with strong, sure movements. She'd wanted to protest, to push him away, but there had been no denying the promise in his eyes or the way he'd made her body respond. She'd woken up hot and achy and unfulfilled.

In the kitchen, she flipped on the small television over her counter and mechanically went through the movements of making coffee. She was reaching for a coffee mug when she went still and then closed the cupboard, her attention riveted on the television. A Washington reporter, elegant in a tailored suit and chic hairstyle, stood in front of the emergency entrance of a local hospital.

"Senior White House advisor, Edwin Zachary, was brought here just past midnight last night with minor injuries, after falling asleep and crashing his car on Post Road. He was treated and released early this morning. There were no other occupants in the car at the time of the accident."

Sara gave a huff of disbelieving laughter. "Fell asleep, my ass," she muttered, and went into the hallway to retrieve the little evening bag she'd carried last night. She couldn't wait to call Lauren and tell her about the incident. If anyone would understand the ramifications of what she had witnessed, Lauren would. Sara might not approve of everything Lauren did to get a story, but the woman took her job as an editor very seriously. She would know the best way for Sara to proceed.

Inside the evening bag she found her wallet, a lipstick, and Rafe Delgado's business card, but no cell phone. It was only then that she recalled dropping it as she'd slammed on the brakes following the accident. Grabbing her keys, she slipped her feet into a pair of flip-flops, opened the door to her fourth-floor apartment and made her way swiftly down the staircase.

Her car was parked just a few doors down from her building, and she unlocked it, crouching to check the floor on the passenger side. The carpeting was black, making it difficult to see anything. Ducking her head to peer beneath the seat, Sara caught sight of her cell phone, wedged between the seat and the center console. Stretching her arm, she was straining to reach the phone when her fingers closed around what felt like a small book. Pulling it free, she saw it was a pocket-sized day planner. She retrieved the cell phone and locked her car, and then carried both items back to her apartment.

Dropping the planner onto the kitchen table, she quickly dialed her editor.

"Hi Lauren, it's Sara Sinclair."

"Sara!" The other woman's voice sounded groggy and surprised. "You do realize it's barely eight o'clock on Sunday morning, don't you?"

"I know. I'm sorry if I woke you up," Sara apologized. "But I was watching the news and there's a breaking story I thought you should know about."

"Go on." Lauren's voice sounded slightly less sleepy.

"Edwin Zachary, the White House advisor—"

"I know who he is," Lauren interrupted. "What about him?"

"He was in a car accident last night. A car accident that I witnessed and stopped to help."

"What happened? Is he okay?"

Sara tucked a strand of hair behind one ear and reached again for a coffee mug. "He was taken to hospital for some minor injuries, but he's going to be fine."

There was a brief silence. "I assume there's a reason you've called to tell me this?"

"The news reports say that he was driving alone and that he fell asleep at the wheel."

"O-kaay…"

Sara could hear the barely veiled impatience in her editor's voice. "Well, that's not what happened. He wasn't alone and he most definitely did not fall asleep at the wheel. He was with a young woman who was definitely not his wife. After I stopped to help, Mr. Zachary asked me to give her a ride home and not to say anything about it. He even tried to give me money to keep quiet."

"Really." Lauren sounded wide-awake now.

"And the reason he crashed his car wasn't because he fell asleep at the wheel, as the news reports claim," Sara continued. "The reason he crashed his car is because the woman was giving him a blow job."

There was a pause, and Sara could almost see Lauren rolling her eyes. "He wouldn't be the first Washington powerhouse to be caught with his pants down. So what are you saying? That you want to expose him?"

Sara frowned. "Lauren, this is big news, especially considering that Edwin Zachary is one of Washington's biggest proponents of family values. He was the first one to publicly denounce Senator Baldwin for having an extramarital affair. Zachary has a serious shot at the presidential candidacy, and yet he's running around doing this? It's incredibly hypocritical. I think this story is worth pursuing."

Lauren sighed. "I agree. Do you know who the woman was? Can we get her to corroborate your story?"

"I know her name is Colette, and I know where she lives."

"Okay. Get her side of the story and then we'll talk. Without that, all we have is your word against his."

Sara nodded. "I'll get it."

"And Sara? This has the makings of a good story, but it's not a done deal. Your interview with Sergeant Delgado? That's a clincher, and that's your priority right now. I don't want you spending a lot of time on the Zachary story. Are we clear?"

Sara barely resisted the urge to hold the phone away from her ear and stare at it in bemusement. She sensed a real reluctance on Lauren's part to pursue the lead, but she didn't understand why. *American Man* magazine wrote about strong men, but they didn't limit those stories to feel-good features. The publication prided itself on showing the good, the bad and the ugly side of power. And Lauren was known to be ruthless when it came to uncovering political scandals. At least, she usually was. Why should this be any different? Sara didn't get it. "I'll call Sergeant Delgado today," she promised.

Which was the last thing she wanted to do, she thought as she hung up the phone. Sara poured herself a cup of coffee and retrieved his card from her evening bag, sitting down at her kitchen table to contemplate it moodily. The dreams she'd had of him were still too fresh in her mind. If she closed her eyes, she could actually feel his lips on hers, warm and hard and demanding. She shivered and opened her eyes.

As business cards went, his was simple and straightforward: heavy white vellum with the Marine Corps logo in one corner and his name, rank and telephone number in bold lettering across the front. Drawing in a fortifying breath, Sara picked up her cell phone and dialed the number. It wasn't yet eight-thirty, and Sara had the perverse hope that she might wake him up.

He picked up on the second ring. "Delgado."

His voice was crisp and alert without the slightest hint of grogginess. The guy had probably been awake for hours. Unbidden, images of him climbing naked out of a rumpled bed swamped Sara's imagination. She could picture it clearly—smooth, tawny skin over sleek muscles, stubble shadowing his strong jaw and throat as he absently rubbed a hand over his corrugated abdomen—

"Hello?" Impatience sharpened his voice, jerking Sara out of her reverie.

"Yes, hi, Sergeant Delgado. This is, um, Sara Sinclair. We met last night at the charity ball?" She winced, wishing she'd used a more authoritative tone, wishing she had waited until later in the day to contact him. He no doubt thought she was desperate, calling him so early on a Sunday morning.

"The journalist." His voice deepened. "I remember."

"I wanted to set up a date—er, an interview—with you for the magazine, and I was wondering when a convenient time might be."

"That all depends," he drawled. "How long do you need?"

The question was perfectly legitimate, yet Sara's rampant imagination imbued it with all kinds of double meaning, no doubt fueled by the dreams she'd had of him. She felt her face grow warm and was grateful that he couldn't see her.

"I'll take whatever you're willing to give me," she finally managed, and nearly groaned at her choice of words. "I mean, however long it takes to get the story. But even if you only have an hour, then that'll be fine, too."

There was a brief silence, as if he were considering. "How does Tuesday work for you?"

Sara hadn't realized until that moment that she'd been holding her breath and now she let it out in a rush of relief. "Yes, that's perfect."

Reluctant to meet Rafe in the intimate setting of a restaurant, she gave him the name of a popular café located at the edge of the sculpture garden on the grounds of the National Mall. The place had a lovely outside seating area, guaranteed to be pleasantly crowded. They agreed to meet there at three o'clock for coffee. Sara hung up and sat back in her chair, considering the prospect of seeing Rafe Delgado again. How would he react when she switched from discussing the Semper Fi Fund to the hostage rescue? She shivered, wishing that the story wasn't so important to Lauren. Wishing that Lauren hadn't asked *her* to conduct the interview.

Her gaze fell on the little black planner that she had found in the car. Frowning, she picked it up and thumbed through it, not recognizing the handwriting scrawled on the pages. The only explanation was that the book had fallen out of Colette's handbag the previous night. The other woman's apartment complex wasn't all that far away. Placing it back on the table, Sara decided she would drop it off later that morning. While she'd been looking forward to a relaxing Sunday of doing nothing, she realized she could use the excuse of returning the book as a perfect way to obtain more information about Colette's involvement with Edwin Zachary. No matter what Lauren said, Sara was certain there was a story there.

SARA STOOD ON THE STEPS of the building where she had dropped Colette off the night before and quickly scanned the list of residents posted near the entry, but didn't see the name *Colette* or even any beginning with the letter *C*. She was unsure what to do next, when an older woman came up the steps.

"Can I help you, dear?" she asked.

Sara turned to her in relief. "Yes, thank you. I'm looking for a—an acquaintance. She left a personal item in my car and I'd like to return it to her, but I'm afraid I only know her first name."

The older woman smiled. "That's no problem. I know everyone in this building and most of the other buildings, as well." She gave a rueful chuckle. "When you've lived here as long as I have, well…let's just say I make a point of getting to know everyone. What's your friend's name?"

"Colette."

"Hmm. Colette." The woman considered for a moment and then finally shook her head. "I don't know anyone here who goes by that name. Are you sure you have the right address?"

Sara nodded. "Yes. I dropped her at this door just last night. She's about twenty-five years old, my height, with long dark hair. Very attractive."

The woman gave her an odd look. "You do know that this is an over-fifty community?"

Taken aback, Sara was momentarily at a loss for words. "No. I had no idea."

"Trust me when I say there are no women in this complex who match that description. The youngest woman here is still twice the age of your friend."

Sara frowned. "Are you sure? I mean, I dropped her off right at this door."

"Did you see her actually enter this building?"

Thinking back, Sara realized she hadn't. She'd been so anxious to get Colette out of her car and get home that she hadn't waited around for the other woman to actually enter the building.

"No, I guess I didn't."

"Well, there you go."

Sara blew out a breath. "I guess so." She forced a bright smile for the other woman. "Well, thank you for your help."

Sara walked back to her car as the older woman disappeared inside the building. With a sigh, she tossed the planner onto the passenger seat and began rummaging through her pocketbook for her keys. She was just getting ready to start the ignition when the planner caught her eye. It had fallen open to the previous day. At the top of the page, in neat handwriting, were the initials E.Z.

Edwin Zachary.

Intrigued, Sara picked the planner up and studied the entry. "What in the world...?"

E.Z.—Prefers relinquishing control. Likes B.J.s, red lipstick, sexy dresses, no panties. Fantasy is sex in public places.

Sara turned the pages until she reached the next weekend, and read the entry for Friday night.

W.W.—Dominant alpha. Likes bondage and rough play. Bring blindfold and silk stockings.

She raised her eyebrows and moved to the next entry.

P.D.—$$$$. Only Four Seasons Hotel. Champagne and caviar. Red-carpet gown with open-toed stilettos. Craves attention/pampering/full-body massages. Foot fetish. Likes doggy-style.

And so it went, entry after entry, weekend after weekend for several consecutive months. Sara returned to the date of the car accident and read the entry once more. Thinking back on what she had witnessed in the car in the moments before the crash, she realized the notation regarding E.Z's preferences was accurate in every detail, right down to Colette's red lipstick. Stunned by the implications of what the little book contained, Sara sat back against the seat and stared blindly through the windshield. No wonder Colette—if that was even her real name—hadn't wanted Sara to know her true address. The law tended to frown upon women who provided sexual services for money, especially when those services were rendered to one of the most powerful men in Washington.

Opening the book again, Sara studied the initials of Colette's other appointments and wondered how many of them were also political powerhouses. The journalist in her shifted restlessly, wanting answers. Wanting to know everything. Did Colette work alone, or was she part of a bigger operation? Had she realized that her planner was missing, and if she did, how badly did she want it back? She must be a little frantic at the thought of it gone. Even now, the reporter in Sara considered the possibilities of pursuing the information, of exposing not only Edwin Zachary, but the other clients in the little book as well.

Breaking this story would certainly guarantee that her name would become nationally known, but suddenly the prospect of being *that* journalist had her heart beating faster. While she'd dreamed of one day uncovering a story of this magnitude, she'd never actually considered the human element behind the headlines. Sex scandals weren't uncommon in Washington, but something like this could destroy a lot of people. Could she accept that kind of responsibility? Did she really want her name connected with that kind of notoriety?

On the other hand, a story like this one could be her

ticket to her own byline on any number of major publications. This was the kind of lead that could make her career.

With a small groan of frustration, Sara was about to close the book when she glimpsed handwriting on the inside of the back cover. Peering closer, she realized it was a telephone number, although she didn't recognize the area code. She doubted that Colette would leave her own telephone number in the book, but what if by some chance the number did belong to her? Retrieving her cell phone, she quickly dialed the number. A woman answered on the third ring.

"This is Juliet." Her voice was low and cultured.

"Hello," Sara responded, her heart beating fast. "I'm looking for Colette."

There was a brief pause. "I'm sorry, who is this?"

"My name is Sara Sinclair. I met Colette last night."

"Really?" The voice sounded amused. "And what makes you think that I know your friend, or her whereabouts?"

"Well," Sara explained, "your number is written in the back of this little black book that she left in my car. I don't know Colette, but I gave her a ride home last night, after she and Edwin Zachary were involved in a car crash. You recognize that name, I'm sure. I can't help but think that Colette might want this particular book back, since it lists her appointments for the next several months. In great detail, I might add. You wouldn't believe what she wrote about Mr. Zachary. Shocking, really."

There was another brief silence and this time, when Juliet responded, her voice was chilling. "I want you to listen carefully, Miss Sinclair. I recommend you burn that book and forget you ever met anyone named Colette. Now be a good girl and hang up the phone right now, and don't call this number again. I'm telling you this for your own good. You don't know what you're dealing with."

Her words caused goose bumps to rise up on Sara's arms, and there was a part of her that was more than tempted to do as the woman directed. She was in over her head.

"Who are you?" she finally asked. "And what are you involved in?"

There were several seconds of silence, when Sara thought the other woman might actually hang up on her. "Who I am isn't important," she finally said. "What *is* important is that you destroy that book and forget whatever you saw written inside."

Sara's glance flicked to the book. She recalled the incident with Edwin Zachary. There was no way she could ever forget what had happened, or how he had tried to bribe her into silence. She might not be an investigative reporter, but every instinct told her she needed to pursue this. Lauren would never forgive her if this story ended up on the evening news courtesy of another reporter. As distasteful as she might personally find the situation, and as much as she might want to take Juliet's advice and hang up the phone, the journalist in her couldn't do it.

"The thing I find most interesting," she mused, as if the other woman hadn't spoken, "is that Colette used initials to identify each of her…appointments. I'm pretty sure that I could figure out whose initials they are. By the way, did I mention that I'm a feature writer for *American Man* magazine?"

There was another silence, longer this time. "I can meet you Tuesday afternoon," Juliet finally responded.

Sara quickly checked her calendar and realized that she'd already agreed to meet with Rafe Delgado on Tuesday afternoon at three o'clock.

"I'm free for lunch on Tuesday, if that works for you," she countered. "How about one o'clock at the Pavilion Cafe? It's located at the west entrance of the National Gallery of Art Sculpture Garden."

"I know where it is. Unfortunately, I'm on a tight schedule and won't have time for lunch. I can meet you at two o'clock, but I can't stay long."

Sara breathed a sigh of relief. At least her meeting with Juliet wouldn't conflict with the time she'd already allotted for her interview with Rafe Delgado.

"That would be fine." She paused uncertainly. "How will I recognize you?"

"Don't worry," Juliet said drily. "I'm sure I'll have no problem finding you. I'll just look for the woman who looks especially...hungry."

As Sara ended the call, she couldn't help but wonder if she'd just made a fatal mistake.

3

SARA ARRIVED AT THE CAFÉ thirty minutes early on Tuesday afternoon, still trying to convince herself that she didn't feel the tiniest bit paranoid or nervous about meeting the mysterious Juliet. She chose an outdoor table where she had a clear view of the walking paths that meandered through the gardens and an easy escape route over the decorative chain that separated the tables from the passersby, if required. She told herself that she was being overly imaginative, but if Juliet really was involved in something illegal, there was no telling what she might be capable of, especially if she considered Sara to be a threat.

The afternoon was clear and cool, scented with the fragrant aroma of freshly brewed coffee from the café. Sara ordered a steaming mug of hot chocolate and sipped it as she watched the people walking past on the sidewalk. A gust of wind rustled through the small trees along the nearest path, catching a handful of golden leaves and swirling them along the ground. Sara's gaze followed them, until her attention was arrested by a man standing beside the nearest garden.

He was leaning against a decorative lamppost and was studying what looked to be a Washington, D.C., guide book, but Sara had the distinct impression that he was watching *her* from behind his dark glasses.

Unsettled, she picked up the menu and pretended to be absorbed in reading it, feeling conspicuously alone despite the comfortable buzz of people all around.

"Miss Sinclair?"

Sara looked up and saw a woman standing by her table. She was older than Sara, probably in her mid fifties, but was one of the most elegant women that she had ever seen, with sleek black hair pulled into a ponytail, and exotic dark eyes. She oozed wealth, wearing boots and a pair of fine woolen slacks, and a leather coat that looked buttery soft.

"Yes, I'm Sara," she said, rising to her feet to take the other woman's extended hand. "Please, sit down."

When Juliet had ordered a cup of coffee, she turned to look at Sara with a shrewd, assessing gaze. "You're younger than I thought you'd be."

"And you're older."

A smile touched the other woman's lips. "Touché. But age is no deterrent to a youthful spirit." She glanced at her watch, an expensive piece of jewelry that glinted with what looked like real diamonds. "Shall we cut to the chase? I have a plane to catch this afternoon and I don't want to be late."

"Of course." Withdrawing the small black book from her purse, Sara laid it on the table, but kept one hand on the cover. "This is the book that Colette left in my car, after she was involved in a car accident with Edwin Zachary. It contains detailed descriptions of Colette's appointments. Salacious descriptions."

Juliet's eyes gleamed. "Were you also involved in the car crash?"

Sara shook her head, watching Juliet closely. The other woman didn't seem the slightest bit fazed by the fact that Colette's book contained potentially damaging information. "No, I wasn't involved. I was driving behind them and let's just say there was a reason why Mr. Zachary was unable to concentrate on his driving," Sara said drily. "Considering what Colette was doing to him, it's a miracle neither of them were killed."

Juliet didn't look surprised or shocked. Instead, a knowing smile curved her lips. "I can only imagine."

Sara picked the book up and as Juliet sipped her coffee, opened it and began to thumb through the pages. "No, I don't think you understand. Here, let me read a sample entry to you."

She flicked her gaze to the other woman's face. Juliet looked patiently composed, but Sara didn't miss how her hands curled tightly around her mug. She gently cleared her throat and began to read.

"'T.F.—Prefers group activities with toys, likes to watch g-g action.'" She slid Juliet a blandly innocent look. "I assume that means girl-girl action."

Juliet briefly raised one hand from her mug. "That's very nice. I've heard enough."

"Wait, there's more. 'Sometimes brings a friend to watch.'" She turned to the next day and quickly scanned the entry. "Oh, this is a good one. It involves food items. I wonder who L.P. is? Hey…isn't there a cabinet member named Lawrence Palmer? Of course, he's pretty old, but you never know…"

"Okay, stop." Juliet leaned across the table, and although her smile never wavered, her dark eyes glittered dangerously. "I don't need to hear anymore."

"Why is your number written in the back of this book?" Sara glanced around to ensure they couldn't be overheard, and lowered her voice. "Are you running a sex ring?"

"Of course not."

"Then what is your connection to Colette? You can't deny that you know her."

"Colette does work for me," the other woman acknowledged, "but it's not what you think."

"Then explain it to me, please, because from where I'm sitting, it certainly looks like she was selling her services."

Juliet sighed and then sat back in her chair to consider Sara for a moment. "I run a business that caters to an exclusive clientele, men who are willing to pay outrageous sums of money to have their fantasies come true."

Sara raised her eyebrows. "Sexual fantasies?"

Juliet gave a dismissive wave of her fingers. "Don't be ridiculous. That would be illegal. We sell fantasies, but our services only include role-playing. Our clients pay a fee for us to create a realistic illusion of romance or seduction, but the girls are expressly prohibited from having sex with the clients." She shrugged. "And if they do, it's strictly consensual and has nothing to do with the business arrangement."

"What's the name of this fantasy-come-true business?" Sara asked drily.

"I called it the Glass Slipper Club," Juliet replied. "Appropriate, don't you think?"

Sara smiled faintly, recalling Colette's observation

that she had resembled Cinderella running from the ball on the night of the car crash. "You're speaking in the past tense."

"Yes, I am. I've wanted to travel for some time now, and I've decided to put the fantasy-come-true business behind me." She gave Sara a meaningful look. "It's not worth ruining my life for."

Sara looked at the other woman, noting the fine webbing of lines around her dark eyes. While there was no question that Juliet was still a beautiful woman, she wasn't getting any younger. Despite her composure, there also seemed to be a vulnerability to her, as if she'd been through some tough times. Did she really want to publicize a story that could destroy her life? Who was Sara to pass judgment on what occurred between consenting adults?

She sighed deeply and passed a hand over her eyes, undecided. After a moment, she pushed the little black book across the table toward Juliet. "Look, why don't you take this?"

Juliet's eyebrows lifted, and Sara thought she saw grudging admiration in their dark depths. "Really? Why would you want me to have it? After all, you could have some of the most powerful men in Washington eating out of your hand with the information this book contains."

Sara gave a self-deprecating smile. "Let's just say that I'm not as hungry as you believed me to be." She gave the book a small nudge. "Please. Take it."

To her astonishment, Juliet pushed back from the table with both hands raised. "Oh, no. Thank you very much, but as I said, I'm putting the fantasy-come-true business behind me."

Sara frowned. "Because of me?"

Juliet laughed. "Goodness, no." She sobered. "I have people much scarier than you to worry about. People who tap my phone and watch my townhouse from the comfort of their big, black sedans."

Sara felt a frisson of alarm shoot through her and she was helpless to prevent herself from glancing over to the spot where she had seen the stranger. He was still there, but now he was talking on his cell phone and looking out over the gardens. Had she imagined him watching her? Was he just another tourist, or did he have a more sinister reason for lingering near the café?

"Who do you think is watching you?" she finally asked, dragging her gaze away from the man.

Juliet shrugged. "The Feds, most likely." Sara watched as she opened her pocketbook and reached inside. "Which means it's time I put the Glass Slipper Club behind me and move on with my life. But you're involved, now, whether you want to be or not."

Sara gave an astonished laugh. "I'm not involved with anything, trust me." She picked up the planner and thrust it toward the other woman. "And if you'll just take this back, I'm going to pretend none of this ever happened."

But Juliet refused to touch the book. "Darling, you became involved the moment you called my number. Even if you hadn't provided your name, the people who are monitoring my phone will have traced the call back to you." She gave Sara a sympathetic smile. "Trust me—you're involved. As for that book, I really don't want it, and since it's unlikely I'll ever see or hear from Colette again, there's really no point in giving it to me."

She glanced at her watch. "It's getting late and I have a plane to catch."

She rose to her feet and Sara did the same. "Where will you go? And what should I do with the book?"

"Personally, I'd love to see the contents of that book printed on the front page of the *Washington Post*, but that's just me." Seeing Sara's expression, Juliet gave a small laugh that had a bitter edge to it. "Don't look so scandalized. Why shouldn't the men involved bear some of the censure? History has shown that it's never them who suffer when their indiscretions are exposed, it's the women." She drew in a deep breath. "As for where I'll go? Someplace far, far from here. I'm sure you recall what happened to the last madam who threatened to expose the names of her clients. Well, that's not going to be me. I've no intention of being found hanging in some backyard shed."

Juliet reached into her pocketbook and pulled out a set of keys, but they slipped through her fingers and dropped onto the flagstoned terrace. Sara bent to retrieve them in the same instant that Juliet also crouched down, and as she reached for the keys, the other woman thrust something into her hand.

"Take this and put it somewhere safe," she whispered fiercely. "A safety deposit box, perhaps."

Sara opened her fingers to see a small computer memory stick in her palm. She frowned. "What is this?"

Juliet smiled and picked up her keys. "Consider it a form of insurance."

"Insurance for what?"

Standing up, Juliet pulled her purse over one shoulder, watching as Sara pushed to her feet. "For your life, my dear." Without another word, she turned and made her way across the crowded terrace and disappeared through the front exit of the café.

Slowly, Sara sat down at the table and considered the memory stick. What secrets did the small device hold, and why did Juliet want to share them with *her?* She considered Juliet's claim that the Feds were watching her. Were they now watching Sara?

Involuntarily, her gaze slid back to the man in the sunglasses. The late-afternoon sun had dipped just low enough to slip beneath the edge of the patio umbrella, and Sara had to shield her eyes to see where he stood. He was still there, but he'd been joined by a woman and a little girl. Even as Sara watched, he lifted the child into his arms, wrapped an arm around the woman's shoulders and walked away, following the graveled path deeper into the gardens.

Sara gave a huff of laughter, feeling a little foolish over her earlier suspicions of being watched. She was letting Juliet's flair for the dramatic get the better of her. There was nobody watching her. Her life was in no danger. Leaning over, Sara opened her handbag and tucked the memory stick into a small, zippered side pocket where it wouldn't get damaged or lost. She'd take a look at it later, when she got back to her apartment.

"Miss Sinclair?"

Snapping upright, Sara blinked and found herself staring at the imposing silhouette of a man. For just an instant, her heart froze in dread. With the sun directly behind him, his features were shadowed, but there was no mistaking that deep voice.

"Sergeant Delgado!"

Sara couldn't keep the relief out of her voice, and she

stood up to greet him. With the sun no longer in her eyes, his dark features came into sharp focus and her breath caught. He wore a black T-shirt with white lettering beneath a black leather jacket, and a pair of jeans that hugged the outline of his muscular thighs. With his tawny skin and raven hair, he looked more than a little dangerous, and Sara was glad she'd chosen the open patio for their interview.

"You looked surprised to see me," he said, and one eyebrow arched inquiringly. "Did I get the time wrong?"

"No, no. I'm just surprised that it's already three o'clock." She indicated the chair that Juliet had recently vacated. "Please, sit down."

He did, indicating her empty mug, and the half-empty coffee cup in front of him. "You've been here for awhile, and I'm apparently not your first appointment."

Sara sat down and signaled to the waitstaff. "I met up with a…friend, but she had to catch a plane. You just missed her." She smiled brightly at him. "What would you like? Coffee? Or maybe a beer?"

"Coffee would be great," he said to the waiter. "Black. And another hot chocolate for the lady."

"How did you know…?"

His eyes fastened on her mouth and he lifted a finger to his lips. "You have a little chocolate, right here."

"Oh!" Mortified, Sara ran her tongue over her lips, and then used her napkin to get rid of the evidence. "Is it gone?"

His attention remained fixed on her mouth with an intensity that made Sara shift uncomfortably in her chair. Something knotted low in her stomach.

"Yeah," he said, his voice a low rasp. "It's gone."

Sara cleared her throat and struggled to compose herself.

"Thank you for meeting me. I really enjoyed listening to you speak at the charity ball."

He inclined his head.

Sara withdrew a small tape recorder and notepad from her pocketbook. "I'm just going to take some notes as we talk, do you mind?"

He shrugged, and Sara thought she detected a glimmer of amusement in his dark eyes. "Not at all. What would you like to talk about?"

"Why don't you tell me about your work with injured marines and the Semper Fi Fund?"

Rafe leaned back in his chair and laced his fingers together over his flat stomach. The zippered opening of his leather jacket fell apart and Sara could read the white lettering on his T-shirt.

You can run, but you'll just die tired.

Unbidden, an image flitted through her head. Rafe pursuing her. Rafe capturing her. Rafe doing things to her that she'd only ever fantasized about. She might die tired, but she'd die happy.

Disconcerted, Sara bent over her little pad of paper and pretended to take notes. The T-shirt was an immediate and vivid reminder of what this man did for a living, what he was committed to. She'd heard the stories about what the men who'd rescued the aid workers had been doing in Pakistan before the kidnapping. While the military had claimed the unit was in the country to provide security for the opening of an all-girls school that the Marine Corps had helped to finance, if the rumors—and Lauren—were to be believed, Rafe had actually been hunting some of the top Taliban leaders as part of an operation so covert the White House denied any knowledge of it.

"I have good friends who were killed or injured in Afghanistan and Iraq," he said, his voice so low that Sara had to strain to hear him. "The Semper Fi Fund helps their families by providing financial assistance when they need it the most."

"But you do more than just provide financial support, isn't that right?"

"We provide emotional support both to the soldier and to his family, that's correct."

Sara listened as Rafe told the story of one soldier who had been severely injured by an improvised explosive device, and had nearly died. To keep his spirits up and offer encouragement, his entire unit lined up each Sunday in Iraq to call him on the telephone.

"That's a wonderful story," Sara agreed. "During your speech at the charity ball the other night, you mentioned that you do work over at the Bethesda Naval Hospital. Can you tell me about that?"

A sardonic smile lifted one corner of Rafe's mouth, but didn't reach his eyes. "I didn't share that information because I'm looking for some kind of validation or recognition. What I do over at the hospital I do because those men are my brothers. They're the true heroes. I just want to raise awareness about their situation."

"You raise money to help their families pay their bills. You spend time with those men and you spend time with their families. I'd say you're the true hero."

Sara didn't miss how his jaw tightened. "Don't mistake me for a nice guy, Miss Sinclair. I'm no hero. If you had any idea what I do for a living, you wouldn't even be sitting here with me."

Drawing a deep breath, Sara didn't allow herself time to think about her next words. If she did, she'd never find the courage to broach the subject. "I think there are three aid workers who would disagree with you. I'm sure that to them, you're the epitome of a hero."

To his credit, his expression never changed. The only indication of his surprise was a barely perceptible tightening of his muscles and a palpable tension in the air between them that Sara couldn't miss, as if his entire body had tightly coiled. The subtle change in him was both frightening and fascinating.

"I don't know what you're talking about." His voice was quiet.

Sara held his dark gaze, although her insides were trembling and her palms were moist. "I think you do. You and your men were in Pakistan last month, presumably to guard dignitaries at the opening of a girls' school in Peshawar, but we both know you were part of a covert operation to hunt the Taliban. Lucky for those women, you were also in a position to bring about their rescue."

Unlacing his hands, Rafe placed them on the table, palms flat against the surface, and leaned forward. Sara found herself trapped in the unyielding blackness of his eyes, unable to look away. When he spoke, his voice was soft and whiskey-rough. "I don't know where you got your information, Miss Sinclair, but if I were you, I'd get your facts straight before publishing a story that has no basis in fact, and could end up being an embarrassment to you and your magazine."

Only the hard glitter in his dark eyes betrayed the

fact he was completely and seriously pissed off. Not that Sara could blame him. If her editor was right and Sergeant Delgado really had been involved in rescuing the aid workers, her story could blow his cover as a covert Special-Operations soldier.

"I have a reliable source who says you were the mastermind behind the rescue," she blurted. "It would make an amazing story if you'd be willing to talk about the rescue. And of course, the magazine would give a huge plug to the Semper Fi Fund."

Rafe stared at her in astonishment for a moment and then laughed softly. "Jesus. I must be getting soft," he muttered, and then pushed to his feet. "The interview is over, Miss Sinclair."

Sara felt her heart drop and she stared at him in dismay. "Wait. What do you mean it's over?"

He was angry. Sara could see it in every pore of his being. But when he spoke, his voice was almost gentle.

"I make it a policy never to speak to journalists, but you seemed so sincerely interested in talking about the Semper Fi Fund that I went against my better judgment and decided to meet with you." He gave a snort of disgust. "But you're not really interested in the injured marines, are you? You'd rather publish a story that's not only classified information, but could put other marines at risk." He stepped back from the table and pushed the chair in. "I'm sorry to disappoint you, Miss Sinclair, but you'll have to get your dirt from someone else."

Sara rose hastily to her feet. "No, wait," she implored as he turned away. He angled his head toward her, his expression unfathomable, and waited.

"I'm sorry," she said quickly. "I don't want to put

anyone in danger. If I promise to keep your identity a secret, would you reconsider?"

His gaze swept over her once more, traveling down and back up her body to rest briefly on her mouth. For an instant, Sara thought she saw something like regret in his face.

"Goodbye, Miss Sinclair."

She watched as he wended his way through the crowded terrace and then disappeared onto the main street. Realizing she was still standing and that several people at nearby tables were watching her with interest, Sara sat back down. The waiter appeared with a small tray and set a mug of hot chocolate down in front of her.

"Don't bother with the coffee," Sara muttered with an apologetic smile. "He's gone."

What had made Lauren think that he would ever agree to talk to her about the rescue? Worse, why had she agreed to ask him about it this way?

She groaned, wishing she could redo the interview, wishing she'd followed her instincts and not pretend to be interested in his charity work. What must he think of her? That she was a dirt-grubbing journalist who would do anything she could to get a story? Sara sighed. She couldn't blame him for walking away. She'd have done the same thing had she been in his shoes. But what was she going to tell Lauren? Her editor had been counting on her.

The fragrant mug of hot chocolate steamed invitingly, but Sara was no longer interested in drinking it. She felt sick to her stomach as she contemplated Lauren's reaction to her disastrous interview. She'd be furious. She'd certainly never invite Sara to another gala event like the charity ball. Instead, she'd be relegated to the ranks of the other junior contributors, writing trivial little articles with no substance.

Gathering up her notepad and the little black book, Sara was preparing to leave when she had the distinct sensation of being watched. Straightening, she glanced at the other patrons, but couldn't find one person who seemed remotely interested in her. Still, the short hairs on the back of her neck tingled with awareness. Trying not to appear obvious, Sara searched the pathways and gardens beyond the cafè, but aside from the normal tourist traffic and business people enjoying the late-autumn afternoon, nothing struck her as unusual.

Still, the feeling of being watched persisted. Unsettled, Sara shoved the book and pad of paper into her pocketbook and placed some money on the table. She didn't look around, but made her way through the cafè and out the front doors. Only when she found herself standing on the busy sidewalk did she breathe a little easier. Nobody was watching her; it was just her overactive imagination. But as she walked in the direction of her car, she couldn't prevent herself from throwing a quick glance over her shoulder.

4

RAFE NEEDED A DRINK. Badly.

Leaving the Pavilion Cafè, he strode along Constitution Avenue until he saw a small pub and ducked inside. He ordered a Guinness and stood at a table near the windows, replaying the interview with Sara Sinclair again in his head.

He hadn't wanted to meet with her, hadn't wanted to be sucked in by the radiance of her smile or the guilelessness in her blue eyes. He'd told himself that nobody could be that sincere, and he'd been right. Sara Sinclair wore her open-faced, Ivory-girl looks like a mask, deceiving those around her into believing that she had only their best interests at heart, while hiding her true nature. In that regard, she was exactly like Ann Lonquist, the woman who'd turned him off journalists.

He could still recall the night he and his men had infiltrated the compound where she and the other aid workers had been held by Taliban forces. Up until that point, the rescue mission had gone smoothly. His team had neutralized the guards positioned around the compound, and within minutes they had found the workers locked in a room deep inside the building.

He and his men had swiftly evaluated the women's physical condition. They were exhausted and frightened, but unharmed. The youngest woman, Ann Lonquist, had clung to him, and Rafe had felt his protective instincts kick into high gear. For just an instant, he'd imagined himself as the big he-man hero and her as the helpless damsel in distress. Then his professional training had kicked in and he'd pushed the fantasy aside. They'd begun working their way out of the compound, using their own bodies to shield the women, when they'd encountered a top Taliban leader. The man had been walking almost absent-mindedly through the corridor, turning an expensive camera over in his hands. The expression of horrified surprise on his face when he rounded the corner and saw Rafe's team of Special Ops soldiers might have been comical if their situation hadn't been so perilous. There was no question in Rafe's mind that he could have eliminated the man without making a sound or rousing any of the other Taliban, but Ann had given a low cry of outrage.

"That's my camera!"

She'd darted forward, but had been restrained by one of Rafe's men. Cursing, Rafe had launched himself at the enemy, just as the man jerked a gun out of his belt and fired wildly in their direction, striking Staff Sergeant Brody in the upper leg.

Then all hell had erupted.

They still might have gotten out unscathed had Ann Lonquist not stopped to retrieve her camera and snap several photos of the now-dead Taliban leader. Rafe had hauled her upward by her arm and literally dragged her alongside him, firing his weapon with his free hand as insurgents pursued them, while she continued clicking the shutter.

"What the hell are you doing?" he'd roared.

"Documenting the rescue," she'd gasped, squirming in his grasp.

Rafe had responded by yanking the camera away and shoving it into a pouch on his belt. "Now move your ass," he'd growled at her, "or I'll damned well leave you here."

Her pretty blue eyes had widened, but she'd snapped her mouth shut and allowed him to shove her ahead of him through the corridors. As he and his men hurried the women toward the exit, gunfire had erupted all around them, and a second man, Sergeant Hager, went down with a muffled cry. Rafe had hauled him up by his flak jacket and supported his weight as they'd made their escape. They'd planted several explosive devices around the compound hours earlier, and now Rafe's men began methodically detonating them. In the ensuing confusion, the team managed to slip into the surrounding darkness with the aid workers, and they hadn't stopped until they were several miles into the surrounding mountains.

Rafe had been forced to carry Hager across the rugged terrain. By the time they'd reached a safe spot to rest, Rafe's entire body had ached with effort. After he'd set the man down, he'd fished through his pouch for his first aid kit, removing Ann's camera and setting it on the ground nearby. The bullet had struck his friend just below the edge of his flak vest, in the side of his abdomen.

"We need to stop the bleeding before we can head to

the extraction point, or he's not going to make it," he'd said grimly. "How is Brody doing?"

"I'm fine," Brody had replied, as another team member wrapped a tourniquet around his injured thigh. "Just a scratch."

A series of blinding flashes had sent Rafe surging to his feet, his weapon drawn. Fury seethed through him when he saw that Ann Lonquist had grabbed her camera from where he'd placed it on the ground, and was busy snapping pictures of their hasty triage. Had he really thought her attractive? With a feral growl, he'd advanced on her.

"Are you that much of an idiot?" he'd hissed, as she backed away. He snatched the camera out of her hands. "What the hell are you doing?"

"D-documenting."

"Just who the hell are you?"

"I—I'm a relief worker." Her voice had sounded high and thin, and Rafe had known she was lying.

"Bullshit. Tell me the truth."

"Fine. I'm a photojournalist," she'd acknowledged in a small voice. "But how else was I going to get my story? I never thought we'd be kidnapped and held hostage."

"Your thoughtless actions nearly got my men killed," he'd said softly, "and now you're determined to advertise our exact location with your fucking camera flash." In disgust, he'd opened the camera and retrieved the small memory card. "What did you plan on doing with these photos?"

He could see from her expression that she'd fully intended to publish them in whatever magazine or newspaper she worked for.

"Jesus," he'd breathed in disgust. "You'd put all our lives at risk for the sake of your story."

"I risked my own life for this story," she retorted. "I've earned those photos."

"The hell you have," he'd snarled.

He hadn't spoken to her again, not during the hike to where a helicopter was waiting to airlift them out, and not when they arrived back at Bagram Air Base. He could barely bring himself to look at her when she'd stiffly asked for the return of her camera. He'd handed it to her—minus the memory card—and then he'd turned and walked away.

His men had survived, but Sergeant Hager had suffered so much internal damage from the bullet he'd taken that he'd been forced to leave the Marine Corps on a medical discharge. Rafe blamed Ann for the fact that he'd lost a good man.

He told himself again that he shouldn't be so surprised—so goddamned disappointed—to realize he'd been right about Sara Sinclair. But he was. There was something about her that appealed to him on a primal level, and it was more than just the ripe lushness of her mouth or her curvy body. There was a kind of innocence to her, a sweet vulnerability that couldn't be hidden no matter how hard she tried to come across as sophisticated and independent. He recalled the look of confusion in her eyes when he'd refused to accept her hand at the charity ball. The memory still made him cringe. He'd behaved like a dick, and all because she'd reminded him a little too much of Ann Lonquist, with her big blue eyes and guileless smile. His initial reaction to Sara had been too reminiscent of his reaction to Ann, only on a bigger scale. He'd been rendered momentarily brainless. He might have rejected her handshake, but he'd spent the night of the ball wondering what it would be like to have her lips on his body, and to fill his hands with her amazing breasts.

He took a hefty swallow of the dark stout, telling himself again that he was an idiot. He might find Sara sexy as hell, but he wasn't stupid enough to get involved with her.

A journalist. A freaking reporter.

Go figure.

He wondered again how she had discovered his involvement in the rescue of the aid workers in Pakistan, and who her source was. There were only a select few people who knew about his role in the rescue, and aside from his own men, most of them were in the higher echelons of the Pentagon.

Rafe was in the process of taking another swig of beer when he paused, the glass raised halfway to his mouth. Sara Sinclair strode past the window of the pub, her coppery hair swinging over her shoulders, her breasts gently bouncing beneath her blue sweater. Rafe barely resisted the urge to press his face to the glass and watch her retreat down the sidewalk. Shaking his head at his own foolishness, he raised his glass again and then paused, the motion arrested by what he saw outside on the sidewalk. A man followed Sara, and as Rafe watched, he gestured to someone on the other side of the street.

Rafe's heart rate kicked up a notch and he swiftly set down the beer and threw some money on the table. Even as part of his brain argued not to get involved, that it was none of his business, he was out the door of the pub before he'd fully realized it. The gesture had been swift and subtle, no more than several flicks of the man's hand, but Rafe recognized the hand signals. He'd used them himself numerous times during close engagements in Afghanistan and Pakistan.

Follow. Intercept. Stay out of sight.

The hand signals were used almost exclusively by the military or law enforcement, but instinct told Rafe the man following Sara was neither. Glancing down the sidewalk, he saw the first man striding purposefully along, keeping five or six pedestrians between himself and his target. Across the street, Rafe saw a second man working his way swiftly through the crowd, presumably to head Sara off.

Even as he watched, Sara turned a corner and disappeared, and the man across the street sprang into action, sprinting into oncoming traffic in order to cross to where she'd vanished down a narrow passageway between buildings. Rafe guessed she was headed for a parking lot on the next street and the alley was a shortcut through. Even if he ran, he wouldn't be able to catch up with Sara before the two men reached her, and every instinct in his body told him this wasn't going to end well for her.

With a muttered curse, he ducked back into the pub and headed for the rear exit, ignoring the surprised exclamation of a waitress as she came around the bar with a tray of drinks.

"Sorry," he muttered, then pushed through the exit door onto a narrow service road and quickly orientated himself. If he sprinted, he could approach the alley from the opposite direction, but he'd need to move fast if he wanted to reach Sara before the two men did. He took off at a dead run, estimating it would take no more than ten seconds to reach the far end of the alleyway.

The lane behind the pub was blocked off and he had to scale the security fence to reach the next road, but it took him no effort to leverage himself over the chain link and drop easily to his feet on the other side. By the time he reached the alley, Sara was a little more than halfway through, seemingly unaware of the two figures who shadowed her.

"Sara," he called, infusing his voice with what he hoped sounded like friendly relief. "There you are! I was afraid I'd missed you."

Sara stopped in her tracks and stared at him, her face expressing her astonishment at seeing him standing there. Behind her, the two men stopped as well.

"Sergeant Delgado," she exclaimed. The alley acted like a wind tunnel, blowing debris around her feet and plastering her hair across her face. She pushed it back with an impatient movement. "What's the matter?"

"Nothing," he said, his glance flicking to the two men. They stood undecided about thirty feet behind Sara, conferring silently. Rafe put an arm around her shoulder, placing himself between her and the men while simultaneously steering her toward the end of the alley. "Friends of yours?" he asked quietly, gesturing toward the men.

Sara looked over her shoulder at the two men in the middle of the alley. A small frown puckered her forehead. "No."

They had almost reached the end of the narrow alley. In another two seconds they would emerge onto the main street, where Rafe could see pedestrians and cars passing by. He propelled Sara out of the alley, and as they turned the corner onto the street, he cast one last look at the two men. Clearly frustrated, one of them kicked savagely at the dirt beneath his feet before they turned and retreated back the way they had come.

"So…why did you come after me?" Sara asked as they walked along the street.

"I just, ah, forgot there was something I did want to tell you, after all."

She looked skeptically at his hand on her shoulder and then up at him, her blue eyes wary. "Really? After the way you left, I can't imagine there's anything you'd want to share with me. You made your feelings perfectly clear."

Afterwards, Rafe could never be sure what made him do it. Maybe it was the expression in her eyes—a vestige of the hurt he'd witnessed at the charity ball when he'd refused to shake her hand. Maybe it was the way she stubbornly set her chin, as if by doing so she could disguise the imperceptible tremble of her lower lip. He only knew that in that instant, he needed to kiss her, to taste her.

"Well, maybe not completely clear," he muttered, and pushed her up against the wall of the nearest building. He swept his gaze over her face. Her lips had parted on a soft "oh" of surprise, and her hands had flattened against his chest, probably to push him away. Before she could form a word of protest, Rafe bent his head and covered her mouth with his own. She went still with shock.

He knew he should pull away, but in the same instant that he realized they were drawing attention from passersby, his brain registered the incredible softness of her lips and the subtle scent that filled his nostrils. She smelled like ginger and honey and he wanted to eat her.

He deepened the kiss, pressing past her lips until he found her tongue with his own and stroked it. She made a small sound in the back of her throat and her fingers no longer splayed flat against his chest. Instead, they curled into the soft leather of his jacket and drew him closer.

She tasted faintly like the hot chocolate she'd drunk earlier, and he angled his head to explore her mouth more fully, feasting on her lush lips. Her mouth had driven him crazy from the first moment he'd seen her at the charity ball, but the reality of kissing her exceeded all of his lustful imaginings. He hadn't meant to kiss her, but he hadn't been able to resist the temptation of her mouth, and what he'd intended to be a brief brushing of their lips had turned into something...more. He needed to regain control of the situation. With supreme effort, he dragged his mouth from Sara's and sucked in a lungful of air.

"Oh," she breathed, and released his jacket, smoothing the bunched leather with her fingers.

Rafe took a step back. Several people walked past and smiled at their public display, no doubt thinking he and Sara were lovers. The woman was safe. Mission complete. If he was smart, he'd turn and walk away—but he made the mistake of looking at Sara. As he watched, she raised her hand and touched her lips with her fingertips, as if she could still feel him there. She appeared dazed, and her hair was tangled from where he'd buried his hands in it. Her breathing was uneven, and she looked exactly the way Rafe felt.

Unbalanced.

"I'm not sorry," he finally said, his voice sounding a little rough. "I've been wanting to do that since I first saw you at the charity ball."

"Oh." Her eyes widened just a bit, and then she pushed herself away from the wall and stepped past him, continuing along the sidewalk. "Is that why you followed me? Because you wanted to kiss me?"

Rafe knew he should tell her about his suspicions that the men in the alley had wanted to harm her, but something made him bite his tongue. He had seen the troubled expression in her eyes when he had directed her attention to the two men, and he suspected she knew why they had been following her. Even now, she couldn't prevent her eyes from scanning the street. Her involuntary response, more than anything else, convinced him that she was in danger. And she knew it.

"Yeah, something like that," he muttered.

She gave a soft sound of disgust. Rafe fell into step beside her. She ignored him as they crossed the street toward a parking lot. He felt her glance flick over him.

"So what is it you really want?" she finally asked, coming to a stop next to a small silver sedan and turning to face him. "After what you said earlier, I have a hard time believing you came back just to—to do that."

Rafe had a hard time believing she had no idea how appealing she was. "There was another reason," he finally said, lying through his teeth. "I've reconsidered doing the interview."

She peered at him, clearly suspicious. "Why?"

He shrugged. "If *you* know I was involved, it stands to reason that others do, too. It's only a matter of time before some journalist decides to run the story, so I'd rather have it done in a way that gets the facts straight while protecting the lives of my men."

He saw the skepticism on her face. "Really? You're willing to let me do the story?"

He paused, considering what he had witnessed earlier. He was convinced the two men following Sara had wanted to hurt her, maybe even kill her. They were probably still lurking somewhere nearby, waiting for an opportunity to finish whatever it was they intended. Sara wouldn't stand a chance against them.

"Yeah," he finally responded. "I'll give you the story—on one condition."

"What is it?" Her voice was wary.

"You need to shadow me 24/7 for the next week. If, after the week is over, you still want to write that story, then I'll tell you everything that happened in Pakistan."

Sara stared at him as though she thought he'd lost his mind, which apparently he had. He didn't want to get involved with this woman, didn't want to get to know her or care about what happened to her. But his gut told him that unless he kept her close, something very bad was going to happen to her.

She tipped her head and considered him doubtfully. "What do you mean…24/7?"

He didn't dare meet her eyes for fear she would see the wolf that lurked just beneath his skin, because he realized that suddenly, he desperately wanted her to accept his offer. So he looked out over the parking lot, keeping his expression bland and his voice neutral. "It means for the next week you're with me day and night. You go where I go."

Her eyebrows shot up and an astonished laugh escaped her. "Why? I don't see any benefit to that. None."

He turned his gaze back to her and shrugged, forcing a nonchalance he was far from feeling. "I just thought that if you spent a week shadowing me, you'd see what I really do, and you'd realize that I'm no hero. Besides, how could you write a story about someone you know nothing about?"

Sara's lips compressed. "How do I know this isn't some devious plot to get me alone so you can—you know." She gestured back toward the alley. "Kiss me."

"You don't."

Considering that he'd just waylaid and accosted her on a public street, the question was more than valid. He could just ask her if there was any reason why someone would want to follow her and perhaps hurt her. But if there was one thing he'd learned in his years of hunting the bad guys, it was never to trust anyone—especially not pretty women with big, blue eyes—without first knowing all the facts. But that didn't mean he couldn't step in to keep her safe.

She chewed her lip, considering his words, and then began rummaging in her purse. "Can you give me a moment, please? I can't just commit to spending a week with you. I have a job, a life! You have no idea what you're asking."

He waited while she punched a number into her cell phone and turned partially away from him, muttering something under her breath that sounded suspiciously like "I must be nuts." He had to agree with her.

He heard snippets of her conversation and guessed that she was talking with her editor, mostly arguing why spending a week in his exclusive company was a bad idea. A very bad idea. But he could tell by the resigned stiffening of her slender shoulders that he had won. She hung up the phone and turned back to him.

"Fine," she said. "I'll do it. When does this one week start?"

He smiled grimly. "Right now."

5

SARA NAVIGATED THE STREETS of the capitol, acutely aware of the dark sports car that followed her. This had to be the nuttiest thing she'd agreed to do in her entire life. Just the thought of spending the next week in Rafe Delgado's company caused a wild churning in her stomach. She'd called Lauren to tell her that she could get the interview, but that it would require her to meet Rafe's unorthodox conditions. Part of her had hoped that Lauren would balk and tell Sara that they didn't need the story that badly.

And part of her had hoped that she wouldn't.

In the end, Lauren had insisted that Sara do whatever she needed to in order to get the story, adding that the additional time in Sergeant Delgado's company would help give the article an authentic, personal touch. Instead of looking triumphant over his success, Rafe had looked grimly determined.

"The agreement is for you to be with me 24/7," he'd reminded her. "No exceptions."

"Yes, I understand," she'd said stiffly. "But I'll need

to go home and pack a bag and at least let my neighbor know that I'll be gone."

And now she found herself driving to her apartment with a dark, dangerous Special-Ops soldier on her tail, and something told her that even if she had a change of heart, she wouldn't get rid of him so easily.

As she turned onto her street and parked on the curb by the front entrance, she wondered what Sergeant Delgado would think of her tiny apartment. Washington rents were obscenely expensive, and even living in a rundown building on the outskirts stretched her finances. A fourth-floor apartment in an old brownstone might not be glamorous, but Sara considered herself fortunate to have it.

She'd moved to the nation's capitol after college, leaving her family and Pennsylvania for the first time in her life, determined to follow her dream of becoming an investigative journalist. Her parents visited every few months, and Sara returned home for most holidays. But the more time she spent in Washington, the less connection she felt to her small hometown. She realized that now Washington had become her home. She'd made friends here. She had a routine, a life. Someday, maybe, she'd be able to afford more than her small apartment, but for now it was sufficient for her needs.

"This is it," she said to Rafe after he pulled in behind her and stepped out onto the sidewalk. "My apartment is on the top floor. There's no elevator."

His eyes gleamed. "I think I can handle four flights of stairs."

Looking at him, Sara had no doubt he could handle forty flights without so much as breaking a sweat. The guy was in supreme physical condition, and if the way his jeans molded his thighs were any indication, he was pure muscle.

"Okay, then," she said.

She was acutely aware of him behind her on the narrow staircase, and found herself a little winded by the time they reached the top.

"Here we are," she said unnecessarily as they reached the fourth floor. Sara stopped outside a door at the top of the stairs and knocked lightly. Seeing Rafe's questioning look, she whispered, "I just want to let my neighbor know that I'll be gone, otherwise she'll worry."

The door opened a crack, and a tiny woman peered out at them, her gray hair in frazzled disarray around her head. When she saw Sara, she smiled and opened the door wider.

"Hello, dear."

"Hi, Mrs. Parker." Sara gestured toward Rafe, who stood just behind her. "This is Sergeant Delgado. I just wanted to let you know that I'm going away for a few days, and I was wondering if you might keep an eye on my apartment for me."

"Why, of course." The woman cast an appraising look at Rafe and her faded blue eyes grew brighter. "Are you going on a romantic getaway, then? If you ask me, it's been far too long since you've been on a proper date."

"Mrs. Parker," Sara protested with an embarrassed laugh, "I'm sure Sergeant Delgado has no interest in my love life."

"Oh, I don't know," mused Rafe, his dark eyes gleaming as he considered Sara. "I think the subject might be…revealing."

"Trust me," she muttered, "you'd be bored to tears.

Thank you, Mrs. Parker. I expect I'll be back in a week or so, but you have my cell phone number if you need to reach me."

Once the older woman had closed her door, Sara proceeded down the hallway to the next apartment and fitted a key into the lock. "Here we are," she said, pushing it open.

She deliberately kept the door open, partly because she felt so jittery being alone with him, mostly because his sheer size made her tiny apartment feel even more cramped and claustrophobic than usual.

"Make yourself comfortable while I throw a few things together," she invited.

She was unaccustomed to having guests, and the sight of Rafe prowling through her small living room gave her a distinct sense of unease. She paused in the doorway of her bedroom and watched as he stood in front of her bookcases and studied the titles there. Did her collection give him any insight into her personality? Her books tended to be a mixture of classics and biographies, with a smattering of self-help titles.

"Excuse me, I'm sorry to bother you," interrupted a woman's voice.

Both Sara and Rafe turned to see Mrs. Parker peering into the apartment.

"Please, come in," Sara said, crossing the living room toward her. "What is it?"

"Well, I forgot to let you know that the landlord sent a repairman over to the building today to fix your balcony." She smiled sweetly. "He was the nicest young man, and he hardly made any noise at all. Why, I probably wouldn't have seen him if I hadn't stepped out onto my own balcony to water my flowers." She laughed and clapped a hand to her chest. "Oh, he gave me a start! I didn't even realize he was there on a ladder until I nearly dripped water on his head."

Sara frowned. "He came to fix *my* balcony? Are you sure?"

Mrs. Parker nodded. "Oh, yes. Well, I just thought you should know. Have fun on your getaway," she called, as she stepped back into the hallway and pulled the apartment door closed behind her.

Sara frowned, and walked over to the sliding doors at the far end of the living room, which opened onto a small, wrought-iron balcony. "That's odd. I had no idea there was anything wrong with the balcony."

She unlocked the doors and slid them open, and was about to step onto the balcony, when Rafe caught her arm. "Wait. Do you use this balcony frequently?"

Sara looked down at his hand on her arm and then up to his face. "I usually have my coffee out here on the weekends, but other than that, not really." She gestured to the tiny café table and matching chairs. "As you can see, there's barely enough room to stretch out your legs, and the view's not exactly spectacular."

Sara's apartment was at the rear of the building, and overlooked a narrow road with a loading dock and several Dumpsters. On the other side of the road was the back side of another apartment building, with iron fire escapes decorating the brick façade.

"Do you mind if I take a look at the repairs before you go out?" Rafe asked.

Bewildered, Sara shook her head. "Not at all. Be my guest."

Rafe poked his head out the door, and examined the balconies to either side of hers. One of them was overflowing with boxes of pink geraniums. "Is this Mrs. Parker's balcony, on the left? Do you think she would mind if I stepped out onto it?"

"Well, I don't know," Sara began uncertainly, but it was too late.

In one smooth movement, Rafe swung himself out the sliding door, holding onto the narrow frame above the sliders. His feet never touched the balcony as he easily levered himself across the space and onto Mrs. Parker's balcony.

"Oh, my God," Sara exclaimed, clutching the door frame and peering out at him. "What are you doing? You could have been killed!"

"Stay where you are," he warned, flicking one glance at her. He crouched down and peered through the railings at the underside of Sara's balcony. He was silent for a long moment, before he stood up and crossed the distance back to her balcony, again using the door frame to support his weight. Only when his feet were safely planted on her living-room floor did Sara breathe again.

"You're absolutely crazy, you do realize that?" she demanded, fear adding sharpness to her voice. "What if you had fallen? You could have been killed! What normal person risks their life to verify a repair job?"

To her astonishment, Rafe just shrugged. "I guess it's just ingrained in me. 'Trust but Verify.'"

"So?" She waited expectantly. "What did you see? The repairs are fine, right?"

For just an instant, she thought she saw something in his eyes—something dangerous—and she shivered. But in the next instant it was gone. "I wouldn't use the balcony until you have your landlord check the work. I think one of the bolts needs tightening, and you wouldn't want to do anything to loosen it more than it already is."

"Is it unsafe?"

"Possibly. More likely the loose bolt will just cause the mortar to break apart, but the balcony could be unstable. Better just to avoid using it until your landlord checks it out."

"Okay, thanks."

"No problem."

But as Sara retreated to her bedroom, she couldn't dispel the feeling that he was hiding something.

RAFE WATCHED SARA close her bedroom door, and raked a hand through his hair, disturbed by what he had seen beneath her balcony. Someone had done some work on the supports, there was no question about it, but their intent had not been to stabilize the balcony, but to undermine it. Two of the supporting bolts had been sheared off, leaving just two bolts to support the balcony. If anyone stepped onto the tiny veranda, the remaining bolts would likely snap, plunging the unfortunate person forty feet to the street below. Just thinking about what could have happened caused Rafe to go cold inside. The fall would have seriously injured Sara—or killed her outright.

Closing the sliding doors, Rafe turned the handle into the locked position, and then dragged her small kitchen table across them, blocking any access to the outside. Hopefully, that would prevent anyone from inadvertently stepping onto the balcony before repairs could be made.

There was no doubt in his mind now that someone was trying to harm Sara. Keeping an eye on her closed door, and his ear cocked for any noise, he moved silently through her apartment, looking for anything that might hint at why her life was in danger. Silently, he opened the drawers of her little antique desk, but found only bills, how-to manuals for her personal electronics and stacks of old Christmas cards. He took care to replace items exactly as he found them. Despite his thorough search, he found nothing to indicate she was involved in anything shady.

In fact, everything in her apartment pointed toward a life that was excruciatingly quiet. A basket of knitting sat next to her sofa, and there was a stack of books and newspapers on the coffee table. She had framed photos everywhere—on the walls and on every shelf and available surface. There were pictures of Sara with babies, children, college friends, and elderly people. However, there were no photos to indicate she had a boyfriend, and Rafe took a quiet satisfaction in the knowledge.

A yoga mat and a Pilates ball were tucked into a corner of the room and she had several exercise DVDs next to the small television. Everything was scrupulously neat and organized. Even her refrigerator was tidy, containing mostly fruit, yogurt and fresh vegetables. The delicate wrought iron wine rack on her counter was empty, and if she had any hard liquor in the apartment, he found no evidence of it. He was beginning to suspect Sara Sinclair had absolutely no vices until he discovered one drawer that contained a substantial stash of expensive gourmet chocolate bars, and he couldn't help smiling.

When her bedroom door finally opened, he was pretending to study a framed photo of her and an older man, sitting under a grass Tiki hut with the blue waters of the Caribbean in the background, holding fruity drinks in their hands.

"That's my dad," she offered, taking the picture from his hands and replacing it on the desk.

"Here, let me take that for you," he said.

She carried an overnight bag over one shoulder, and her pocketbook and a laptop case in her other hand.

"It's okay," she demurred, "I've got it."

Ignoring her protests, he took both the overnight bag and the laptop from her and then pretended to stagger beneath the weight. "Christ," he muttered, "what do you have in here?"

Her overnight bag wasn't large, but it weighed a ton.

"Just a few essentials," she said breezily. "This will only get me through the next few days. I didn't want to pack an entire suitcase, so I figured I'd come back in a couple of days to pick up some new clothes."

"Sure," he grunted, wondering what she could possibly have in the bag that would only get her through a few days. If he didn't know better, he'd have sworn she'd packed a flak vest, combat boots and a loaded ammunition belt in that little bag.

She preceded him to the door of the apartment, stopping when she saw the kitchen table pushed up against the sliding doors. She didn't say anything, but when she turned to look at him, he saw she'd gone a little pale.

"It's just a precaution," he assured her. "I didn't want you to forget that it's unsafe and mistakenly step onto the balcony."

"Thank you."

When they stepped outside, it was almost dark. Sara began walking toward her car, and Rafe stopped her with a hand on her arm.

"Leave your car here. You can ride with me."

She whirled back toward him, twin spots of color riding high on her cheekbones. "Okay, you know what? This is beginning to feel less like a journalistic opportunity and more like enforced captivity." She gestured impatiently toward her car. "Why can't I just bring my car and park it at your place? I need my car, Sergeant. I don't mind shadowing you for the next week, but I absolutely refuse to be dependent upon you. What if our arrangement doesn't work out? What if I want to leave?"

Her entire stance was defensive, as if she fully expected him to argue with her. Rafe noted the small telltale signs that signaled her willingness to fight him on this issue, or turn and walk away from him altogether. Even in the indistinct light he could see how her pupils had dilated, turning her blue eyes almost black. Her respiration had increased and her hands curled into fists at her sides. Every muscle in her body was tightly coiled. If he gave her the slightest argument, she'd run.

"Okay," he said easily. "If it makes you feel more comfortable, I want you to take your own car."

She looked at him doubtfully, and he could almost see the resistance ebb from her body. "Really?"

"Absolutely. Do you have a GPS, just in case you lose me in traffic?"

"Yes."

He gave her the address and then stowed her gear in the back seat of her sedan. He would have preferred to have her in his car with him. If someone did decide to follow them, it would be harder to lose them if Sara was in a separate vehicle.

"You have my cell phone number," he reminded her. "My place is about forty minutes from here, near the Quantico base, so if you lose me in traffic, don't hesitate to give me a call. I'll pull over until you catch up."

"I'll be fine," she assured him. "Believe it or not, I can look out for myself. I don't need a man, even one as big and capable as you, to take care of me."

As Rafe watched her climb into her car, he very much doubted it. Sara Sinclair had no clue how much she needed him.

6

AS IT TURNED OUT, Sara managed to keep up with him as he drove along the darkened streets of the capitol and merged onto the highway that would take them south to Quantico. Most of Rafe's military buddies lived on the base, but Rafe had chosen to rent a place in the nearby town of Triangle. He preferred the quiet neighborhood that bordered a vast swath of protected forest to the noisy energy of the Marine Corps base. His entire life was the Corps, and while he wouldn't have it any other way, he appreciated the solitude of the townhouse when he returned home from overseas deployments and missions.

Although he worked as part of a five-man Special-Ops unit, he had a reputation for being something of a loner, which didn't bother him. While the other guys on the team had formed some pretty tight friendships, he tended to remain a little detached. He'd give his life for any one of them, even the newest and youngest member, Corporal Josh Legatowicz, or Lego, as the team called him, who was far more cocky than he had a right to be, but Rafe preferred to keep to himself when he was on leave.

He turned on to the road that led to the small townhouse complex, watching Sara's car in his rearview mirror. The neighborhood was quiet, and he didn't see any signs that car had been followed, although he wouldn't take the chance of her car being spotted in his driveway. Pulling up to the curb in front of the three-story townhouse, he motioned to Sara. She came alongside and rolled down her window, peering up at him in the gloom.

"Pull into the garage," he directed her, indicating the one-car space on the ground floor of the townhouse.

"But what about your car?" she protested.

"It'll be fine," he assured her.

He carried her two bags into the townhouse, acutely conscious of her standing beside him. While her apartment had been neat, his was positively Spartan, with gleaming hardwood floors and walls that were almost entirely bare of pictures or artwork. There was a rug on the living-room floor, but the only furniture was an ancient distressed-leather sofa and club chair that he'd inherited from an uncle, a side table and matching coffee table and a lamp. There was a gas fireplace on one wall and a built-in flat-screen television over the mantel. He had a decent sound system and some pictures of himself and his Marine Corps buddies on a shelf, but looking at his home through Sara's eyes, he realized how empty the place must look. His mother had sent him some decorative pillows and throws, but they were still packed away somewhere. He needed to dig them out, he thought absently.

"There's a guest bedroom at the top of the stairs,"

he said, and led the way up the staircase to the second floor. He opened the door of the spare room that doubled as his office and flipped on the light switch. There was a queen-sized bed with a Red Sox bedspread under the windows, and a desk where he kept his computer and electronics. "It's pretty utilitarian, but the bed is comfortable and you have your own bathroom."

Walking into the room, he showed her the small bath. "I keep extra towels, shampoo and soap in the closet, so help yourself to whatever you need."

"Thanks," she murmured, and watched as he deposited her bags on the bed.

He needed to get out of the bedroom because he was starting to have images of her lying across the Red Sox logo. Naked.

He'd never felt this way before, as though he was on the brink of losing control. Sara stood watching him from the center of the room. Did she have any idea of his thoughts? Could she sense how close he was to ignoring the warning sirens going off in his head and doing something they would both regret? Raking a hand across his hair, he turned and walked out of the room. Away from temptation, but not away from his imagination, which continued to roll Technicolor images of Sara in his house. In his shower. In his bed.

She followed him down the staircase and through the living room. "Geez, what time is it?" she asked, walking into the kitchen to pull out a stool from the center island and climb up. "I'm starving."

"Why don't I run out and grab us a pizza?" he offered, anxious for an excuse to get away from her and get his head together. "There's a great little place just outside the base. If I go pick it up, I could be back in a half hour."

"Mmm. That sounds good." She slanted him a teasing look. "But is it okay for me to stay here without you? I mean, technically, our 24/7 agreement means I should go with you, right?"

Rafe felt his lips pull into a reluctant smile. "You'll be fine here without me. Just lock the door behind me, okay?"

RAFE REALIZED HE HAD NO IDEA what kind of pizza Sara liked, so he ordered a plain cheese, a meat-lovers, and a veggie, and then stopped at a convenience store and grabbed a six-pack of beer and a bottle of Chianti, and then on impulse, a box of hot chocolate mix. By the time he returned to the apartment, he realized he'd been gone for over an hour.

Unlocking the door to the townhouse, he didn't see Sara in the living room or in the kitchen. He deposited the pizza and groceries on the kitchen island and walked to the foot of the staircase, intending to knock on her door to let her know he had returned, when he heard the shower going. He backed away, the former images of her rushing back through his head.

"Oh, man," he muttered. "I am losing it big-time."

Granted, it had been a while since he'd had sex, but he didn't think he'd reached the point where he would jump a woman he barely knew. A woman who'd trusted him when he'd promised that he had no ulterior motives in asking her to spend a week in his company.

Walking back into the kitchen, he cracked a beer and was in the process of putting the remaining bottles into the fridge when his gaze fell on Sara's purse sitting in the living room. He could still hear the water running in the guest bathroom. Moving quickly, he brought the handbag over to the kitchen island and began methodically to go through the items inside. He needed to know why someone was following her, why someone would deliberately tamper with her balcony in a manner that could have easily resulted in her death.

Pulling out her cell phone, he skimmed through her recent calls and text messages, but didn't see anything suspicious. He set aside a small pouch of cosmetics and a disk of birth-control pills and flipped through the small notepad she had used during their brief, failed interview. Aside from the few notes she had scribbled during their conversation, the notepad was blank.

Finally, he pulled out a small black date planner. Setting it aside, he ran his hand along the inside of the empty handbag to ensure he hadn't missed anything. Feeling a small lump, he opened a zippered side pocket and found a computer memory stick. Normally, he would access the stick and look at the information it contained, but his computer was in Sara's room. There was no way he would go in there while she was in the shower. Maybe later, if the opportunity arose. Replacing the memory stick, he picked up the planner and thumbed through it, scanning the hand-written entries.

"What the…?" he muttered aloud.

Rafe read several of the entries at the beginning of the book, and then flipped rapidly through the pages. He'd seen and done things in his life that would horrify most decent people. In fact, he'd thought he was long past the point where anything could shock or even surprise him, but he realized he'd been wrong.

He closed the book, a deep disquiet settling into his

soul. He knew damned well what the entries meant and what the book implied, yet he couldn't reconcile the reality of it with what he knew about Sara Sinclair. She'd disappointed him when she'd pressed him for information about the rescue of the aid workers, but he at least understood her reasons for doing so.

But this…

Never in a million years would he have thought a woman like Sara Sinclair would be capable of selling her body, of engaging in sex with complete strangers for money. Reluctantly, he picked up the little book again and reread several of the sordid entries. He closed his eyes against the unwelcome images that swam through his mind, but all he could picture was Sara—sweet, clean, wholesome Sara—with some sweating, panting animal on top of her, subjecting her to whatever deviant sexual desires he had. The bleakness of it made him feel ill. Curling his hand around the book, he struggled to control his rising anger, when all he really wanted to do was to destroy something, to lash out and smash something.

Anything.

He couldn't remember the last time he'd felt such impotent rage. Sucking in a deep breath, Rafe forced himself to relax and think logically. He couldn't let emotions rule his actions. As the red haze began to subside and he considered what he had seen, doubt began to replace his anger. There was something about the book that didn't seem right, but he couldn't put his finger on it. Turning back to her pocketbook, he began digging through it once more, looking for the notepad she'd used during their interview.

"What are you doing?"

He whirled from the counter to see Sara standing several feet away. Her wet hair hung over her shoulders and she'd scrubbed her face clean of all cosmetics. She'd changed into a pair of jeans and a green pullover sweater, and she looked absurdly young. She was staring at him now with a mixture of confusion and dawning horror, and Rafe knew how it must look. He had one hand inside her open purse, and half of the contents were still on the counter. Worse, he had the little black planner clutched in his other hand. So much for covert operations.

"Oh, my God," she breathed.

She darted forward and tried to snatch the book from him, but he held it out of reach.

"How dare you?" she demanded, her voice low and furious. "How dare you go through my personal things? What gives you the *right?*"

"How about you telling me what the hell this is all about?" he asked grimly, indicating the planner. "Jesus, Sara! Please say that this is a joke."

"No," she bit out. "It's not a joke."

This time, when she reached up for the book, he let her take it. He watched as she scooped up her belongings and shoved them back in her pocketbook. Then, throwing him a level, hostile look, she marched back up the stairs and he heard the door to her room close with a decisive *click.*

"Goddamn." He scrubbed a hand over his face and debated between going after her or giving her some time to cool off. But he was unprepared when she came back down the stairs wearing her jacket and carrying her overnight bag and laptop case. She cast him one defiant glare before stalking past him.

"Whoa," he said and caught her by the arm, halting her progress. "What's going on? Where are you going?"

She stared pointedly at his hand on her arm. "Let go of me. I can't stay here with you. Not for a week. Not for another minute."

"Why?" he demanded. "Because I discovered your secret?"

She looked at him, then, her eyes flashing. "You went through my *purse*. Why would you do that?"

"Because I knew you were hiding something." He nodded toward her handbag. "And I was right."

"I'm not hiding anything."

"Oh no? How do you explain what's in that book?"

She was silent for a moment, and he could see her struggling to form a response.

"What's the matter?" he asked softly. "Cat got your tongue? Or did you forget that you have an *appointment* tonight?" He squinted and pretended to think. "Let's see…is it with the guy who likes it rough, or the one who likes to do it doggy-style while feeding you caviar? Is that how you met your 'reliable source'? You know, the one who told you I was involved in the rescue of the aid workers?"

"What?" She stared at him, her expression bemused. "You think…oh, my God."

To his astonishment, she started to laugh and then immediately clapped a hand over her mouth.

"What's so funny?" he growled. "I don't think there's anything particularly amusing about high-risk sex."

He watched as warm color seeped up her neck and into her face. "You actually think that I'm capable of doing the things written in that book?" she finally asked. "I don't know whether to be flattered or insulted."

"Trust me, I didn't mean it as a compliment. But the reality is, I don't know what you're capable of."

"Not that!" she exclaimed, and set her bags on the floor. "Rafe, the planner doesn't belong to me. I didn't write those entries, and I would never do those things." A smile quirked one corner of her mouth. "At least, not with just anyone."

Rafe's body responded instantly to the images her words conjured up—Sara, doing those things with *him*. Driving him crazy. Making him lose control.

Pushing the erotic visions aside, he realized it was the first time she'd addressed him as anything other than Sergeant Delgado, and he wished he didn't like the way his name sounded coming from her mouth so much.

"So if the book doesn't belong to you, then why do you have it?" he asked brusquely.

She studied him for a moment, obviously debating whether to trust him. Finally, she walked over to the kitchen island and opened her handbag, pulling the little black book out and laying it on the counter. "I only know that it belongs to a woman named Colette. I gave her a ride home after the charity ball the other night, and she must have dropped this when she was getting out of my car. But until that night, I'd never seen her before."

Rafe came to stand beside her. The top of her head came to his chin, and he could smell the ginger-honey scent of her shampoo. Her hair was beginning to dry in soft, curling tendrils around her shoulders, and he had to fight the urge to pick up a strand and rub it between his fingers.

"May I?" he asked, indicating the small notepad that rested inside her purse.

She handed it to him, and he opened it to where she had taken notes during their brief interview. Opening the little black book, he placed them side by side on the counter. Whereas Sara's writing was neat and elegant, the entries in the planner were written in a loopy scrawl and embellished with smiley faces and hearts.

"Definitely not the same writing," he mused.

She gave him a tolerant look. "As I said, the book doesn't belong to me."

"So who is this Colette, and how did you end up giving her a ride home? Was she at the charity ball? Did her, uh, escort ditch her?"

"Not exactly," Sara hedged. She indicated the three pizza boxes stacked on the counter and an amused smile touched her mouth. "Are you expecting company?"

"No, but I wasn't sure what kind of pizza you like, so I got a variety." He leaned against the counter and crossed his arms. "You're not going to change the subject, Sara. How did Colette end up in your car?"

Without looking at him, Sara opened each of the boxes, finally settling on the veggie pizza. He watched as she pulled a warm slice free and took a delicate bite from the end.

"Mmm," she exclaimed, closing her eyes briefly in appreciation. "Delicious. I can't remember the last time I had pizza this good."

Rafe watched as she caught a trace of errant sauce on her lips with the pink tip of her tongue. His body stirred in reaction.

"I'm waiting," he said, his voice rougher than he'd intended.

She swiped her mouth with her fingertips and looked at him. "Okay, fine. But you need to promise me that the information I'm about to tell you goes no farther than this room. *Promise.*"

Rafe didn't like making promises when he had no idea what he was committing to, but he nodded curtly. "I promise."

Sara reluctantly set the slice of pizza down. "I was driving home on the night of the charity ball and got behind an expensive little sports car out on Post Road."

Rafe watched in fascination as warm color seeped into her face, and for a moment he didn't think she would continue. "And…?" he prodded.

"And it was pretty obvious what was going on in the car while they were driving."

"Can you be more specific?" Rafe asked.

She gestured vaguely. "You know…her mouth was on him."

"She was kissing him?" he asked helpfully.

Sara gave him a baleful look. "Are you really going to make me spell it out for you? Yes, she was kissing him, in a manner of speaking. But not on his lips, if you know what I mean."

"Ah…" Rafe found her obvious discomfort both amusing and endearing. He couldn't remember the last time he'd seen a woman blush.

"Okay, so what else? You followed them?"

"Yes. Their car crashed into a tree and I stopped to see if I could help. But then I realized who was driving, and I wished that I hadn't stopped. And this is where your promise to keep this information confidential comes in."

"I already gave you my word."

There was a momentary pause. "The driver was Edwin Zachary."

For the second time in less than hour, Rafe discovered that he could still be shocked. Zachary's name was the last one he'd expected to hear. While there were plenty of politicians involved in sleazy backroom deals and sexual scandals, Edwin Zachary had always seemed to be above that. He and his wife were cornerstones of Washington, D.C. society, and Zachary was known for his firm sense of ethics. He was also rumored to be a strong contender for the next presidential campaign. Why would he risk everything for sex with a prostitute? It made no sense to Rafe.

"Go on," he encouraged her. "What happened then?"

Sara described how Edwin had asked her to drive Colette home, and how he had offered her money and requested that she keep the incident a secret.

"I refused the money, but I couldn't just leave Colette there," Sara said. "So I drove her home and then found the planner on the floor of my car the next morning. I went back to where I had dropped her off, but was told that nobody lives there who fits her description."

Rafe pulled a second beer from the refrigerator and opened it. He handed it to Sara before taking a long swallow from his own bottle. He found it hard to believe that the incident might have endangered Sara's life, but he couldn't discount the possibility that Edwin Zachary was trying to silence her, especially since she had refused to accept his money. It would have been simple enough for him to write down her license-plate number and then send someone after her.

"Is that everything?" he asked grimly. She hesitated, and he could see that she was debating on whether or not to share more with him. "C'mon, Sara. Spill."

"There's a phone number in the back of the planner, so I dialed it, but it didn't belong to Colette. I spoke with a woman named Juliet who said she runs a business that makes fantasies come true."

Rafe snorted. "I bet."

"Of course she swore that her employees—for lack of a better word—are prohibited from having sex with their clients. She insisted that if they do, then it's consensual and has nothing to do with the Glass Slipper Club. I mean, *had* nothing to do with the club."

Rafe made a grunting sound. "What do you mean, 'had nothing to do with the club'?"

"Juliet told me that she thinks the Feds are watching her and she's leaving the country for a while. The club apparently isn't in operation anymore."

Everything fell into place for Rafe. There was no question in his mind that Sara's life was in danger. The only remaining question was whether Edwin Zachary was behind it. The only other person who might have a motive to remove Sara from the picture was Juliet, especially if she knew that Sara was a journalist and could potentially expose her to the world.

Rafe recalled what had happened the last time the press had exposed a Washington madam; she had been found hanging by her neck. Juliet might feel threatened enough to decide Sara was too much of a risk. Not only to Juliet's questionable business, but to her very life.

7

SARA WATCHED RAFE OVER the rim of her beer bottle. He looked every inch as dangerous as Lauren had warned. Picking up the black book, he flipped to where Juliet's phone number was written and pulled out his cell phone.

"What are you doing?" Sara asked, but was afraid that she already knew. She watched him, wondering if she should tell him about the jump stick that Juliet had given her. He hadn't mentioned it to her, so she had to assume that he hadn't found it during his search of her handbag. She'd told him everything else that had happened, so why not share that, as well? Sara knew instinctively that she could trust him—but until she could look at the contents of the memory stick, she decided to keep its existence a secret. What had Juliet called it—an insurance policy? If that was true, it would be better to keep it under wraps until she knew what information it contained.

Rafe's black eyes glittered as he held his cell phone to his ear. He regarded her with one finger over his mouth. "Shh. Don't say a word." He listened for several moments, but then closed the phone with a frustrated snap. "The number is no longer in service."

"That would support what Juliet said about getting out of the business, right?" Sara asked.

"Possibly." He considered her for a long moment and then blew out a hard breath. "C'mon, let's take our pizza into the other room. I'll start a fire and see if there's anything good on television."

Without waiting for her response, he scooped up two of the pizza boxes and his beer and retreated to the living room, leaving her alone in the kitchen. Sara couldn't believe that he had actually thought the little black planner belonged to her. Recalling his reaction, butterflies swarmed in her stomach. When he'd demanded to know who she was going to meet, and then recited some of the sexual activities that had been written in the book, only one thought had gone through Sara's mind—what would it be like to do those things with him? She shivered.

Picking up her beer, Sara followed Rafe into the living room and sat at one end of the roomy sofa. She watched his easy movements as he lit a fire and then clicked a remote through a series of channels until he finally settled on a James Bond movie. With a questioning glance in her direction, he sat down at the other end of the sofa.

"I thought you were starving," he commented, indicating her mostly uneaten slice of pizza.

"I guess not as much as I thought."

Leaning forward, he braced his forearms on his knees and laced his hands together. "Look, I apologize for going through your personal things. I didn't want to invade your privacy, but something happened today that you need to know about."

Sara gave rueful laugh. From the time she had come across the accident with Edwin Zachary, it seemed her life hadn't been the same. "A lot of things happened today, Rafe. At this point, nothing would surprise me, so let's hear it."

"Do you recall the two men in the alley earlier today? I think they were following you."

Sara recalled the sense of being watched while sitting at the café and knew instinctively that Rafe was telling the truth. Someone *had* been watching her. She'd felt it. But she hadn't realized she'd been followed back to the alley. Not until Rafe had asked if she knew the men had she even realized anyone was behind her. At the time, she *had* wondered if they'd intentionally followed her, but then Rafe had kissed her and all thoughts of the two men had vanished. The thought of someone deliberately stalking her, slinking behind her like a hungry wolf, made her feel a little ill. Especially since she knew better. She'd lived in Washington for three years, and she was usually pretty safety-conscious. But it had been daylight, and she'd been so close to the sculpture gardens and the bustle of Independence Avenue, that she'd felt safe.

Sara nearly groaned aloud. She'd believed him when he'd told her that he'd wanted to kiss her since the night of the charity ball. Worse, she'd kissed him back and had even allowed herself to fantasize about what it might be like to do more than just kiss Rafe Delgado. Now she knew he'd kissed her only as a pretext. Maybe he didn't even find her attractive.

Sara gave him a rueful look. "So you only came after me to protect me."

He shrugged. "I was just going on instinct."

The way he watched her, as if he could read her thoughts, was a little unnerving, but Sara found she couldn't look away. She realized that, up close, his eyes weren't actually black, but a brown so deep and dark that she could only barely discern his pupils. His lashes were thick and lush for a man, and his mouth… Good Lord, his mouth looked as if it had been sculpted purely for pleasure, and Sara had a nearly overwhelming urge to rub her own against it.

"You kissed me just in case they were still watching us." She looked down at his hands, loosely linked between his knees, at the strong wrists and fingers, and the dusting of dark hair along his skin. She gave a huff of self-deprecating laughter. "I'll give you credit for a realistic performance. You even had me fooled."

"Is that what you think?" he finally asked, his voice low and rough. "That I kissed you just for show?"

"Didn't you?"

To her astonishment, he slid a warm hand along her jaw, his fingers tangling in her damp hair. His expression was taut and his eyes glittered hotly.

"I meant what I said after I kissed you," he said softly. "I'd been wanting to do that since I first saw you at the ball."

As if to emphasize his words, his gaze fastened on her mouth and his head dipped toward hers. Sara was only vaguely aware of moving toward him.

"I'm sorry," he muttered, "but I have to…"

He didn't finish, and the last thing she saw before

her lashes drifted closed, was his delectable mouth descending toward hers.

His lips were warm and firm and so sinfully talented that Sara gave a small murmur of pleasure and eased closer. Her hands crept to his arms, feeling the hard thrust of muscles beneath the soft fabric of his jersey. He took his time, teasing and tasting her, until Sara slid her hands upward, over the slope of his shoulders until she encountered the hot, satiny skin at the nape of his neck.

He made a small growling sound of encouragement and then both hands were cradling her head, tilting her face for the full, sensual assault of his lips and tongue against her own. He tasted faintly of beer and smelled like crisp soap and a hint of something spicy. His fingers against her face were strong and warm, and the sensation of his tongue stroking her own caused a heat wave of desire to crash over her.

She'd had an immediate physical reaction to Rafe Delgado the first time she saw him, but the reality of touching him and having his mouth on hers was beyond anything she could have imagined. Sara didn't consider herself a prude. Far from it, actually. But her former boyfriends had been writers or musicians, and had been more dreamy than dangerous, more moody than masculine. But there was nothing tempered or hesitant about Rafe's kisses. He plundered her mouth as his fingers buried themselves in her damp hair and held her still.

He eased her back against the arm of the sofa and she went willingly, drawing him down on top of her until the delicious weight of his body pinned her against the cool leather cushions. He lifted his head briefly to search her face with eyes that glittered hotly in his dark face.

"Okay?" he murmured, his breathing uneven.

"Oh, yeah..." she whispered, and drew his head back down to hers, spearing her fingers through his short hair and reveling in the velvety texture and the warmth of his scalp. Shifting restlessly beneath him, she managed to curl one leg around the hard length of his thigh and he settled into the cradle of her hips as if he had been made to fit there.

She wound her arms around him, stroking the long muscles of his back until she encountered the bottom edge of his shirt, and slid her hands beneath it. His skin was like hot silk beneath her fingers and she stroked higher, admiring the strength and power of his body.

He tore his mouth from hers and dragged his lips along the line of her jaw until he reached the tender skin beneath her ear, and then he bit her flesh lightly before soothing it with his tongue. Sara shivered, feeling a bolt of pure heat lash through her. She throbbed where his hips pressed against hers and she had to resist the urge to rub herself against him.

As if sensing her need to get even closer, Rafe slid a hand along the slope of her shoulder and downward, and then boldly cupped a breast beneath the soft fabric of her sweater. Sara gasped as he gently cupped and kneaded her, then rubbed his thumb across her hardened nipple.

"You feel great," he rasped, and skated his tongue lightly along the curve of her ear.

Sara opened her eyes, thrilling at the sight of his broad shoulders and dark head bent over her, feeling his big hand caress her as she arched helplessly upward. The small part of her brain still capable of coherent thought argued that she knew next to nothing about Rafe Delgado. She'd never had sex with a stranger. In fact, she'd never even considered becoming intimate with someone with whom she wasn't in a committed relationship, but she was contemplating it now.

His hand followed the curve of her waist to her hip, and then swept beneath the edge of her sweater to smooth over the bare skin of her stomach. When he cupped her breast again, there was only the fragile barrier of her bra separating his palm from her skin.

"You're so damned soft," he muttered, and before Sara realized his intent, he pushed the sweater up and bent his head to draw on her nipple through the sheer fabric of the undergarment.

The moist heat of his mouth caused a rush of wetness to her center, where she ached for him. She gave an inarticulate cry of pleasure and held his head to her breast, even daring to take his earlobe between her teeth and nibble gently. Her action seemed to arouse him further, and he pushed her bra down until he freed one breast.

"Gorgeous," he breathed in a reverent tone, and covered her with his hand, teasing and caressing the beaded tip until Sara writhed beneath him. Only when she moaned softly did he bend his head and close his mouth around her, drawing sharply on her nipple.

Sara stroked her cheek against the rough velvet of his short hair, breathing in his scent. She pressed upward, feeling the hard thrust of his arousal behind the zipper of his jeans. She'd never been so turned on or so acutely aware of her own body. Every nerve ending was vibrantly alive and cried out for fulfillment.

When he released her breast and began to trace a path downward, she sank back against the leather cushions and let the pleasure of his touch consume her. His hands reached the waistband of her jeans, and she held her breath, waiting for him to work the fastening. Instead, he abruptly pulled away from her. Cool air wafted across her bare skin and Sara opened her eyes in bewilderment. He sat up with her leg still curved around his hips, and scrubbed his hands over his face. His breath came in aggravated surges. Disoriented, Sara adjusted her clothing as Rafe carefully disentangled himself from her legs before standing up.

"We need to talk," he finally said, sliding her a meaningful look. "There's nothing I want more than to take you right here, right now. But I don't want you to think the only reason I asked you to stay with me for the next week is so that I can have sex with you."

Right now, at this moment, Sara couldn't think of a better reason to stay with Rafe. Her breasts ached and her body thrummed with unfulfilled need, but she pushed herself to a sitting position and tried to focus on what he was saying…when what she really wanted to do was reach for him and encourage him to finish what he'd started. Swiping her hair back from her eyes, she turned to face him, self-conscious and wary. His expression was grim. Sara couldn't imagine what must be going through his head.

SARA STARED AT HIM with eyes that were still hazy with pleasure, her hair tangled around her face and her sweetly decadent mouth swollen from his kisses. More than anything, he wanted to drag her jeans from her body and bury himself in her welcoming heat. He'd been so close to doing just that, when some last vestige of sanity had surfaced. Even then, he'd been tempted to ignore the warning sirens going off in his head. Instead, he'd drawn on every bit of restraint he had, using his marine training to rein in the rampant lust that had consumed him. He'd backed off, but it had been several long, uncomfortable moments before the red haze had cleared enough for him to control his rioting impulses.

"I know why you asked me to shadow you for the next week," she said, her voice soft. "Because everything I said about you is true, and this only proves it."

He slanted her a questioning look, trying not to notice how sexy she looked, or the way she regarded him as if he was her own personal hero. "What do you mean?"

"Your insistence that I shadow you for a week has nothing to do with my writing a story about you. You made my being here a condition of writing the story because you wanted to protect me. How is that not heroic?"

She was right; he couldn't give a shit about her story. In fact, despite what he'd promised Sara to get her here, he'd never planned to answer her questions about the rescue at all. Did that make him a hero?

"Sara, listen to me," he said carefully. "There was something about those guys who were following you. They were hit men." He drew in a deep breath. "I'm almost certain they wanted to kill you."

Sara blinked at him, uncomprehending. "What?"

He sat down beside her, reminding himself that she had no experience with the dark underbelly of society. She'd probably never had anyone say so much as a cross word to her, never mind deliberately try to harm her.

"Why would you think that?" she asked in bewilderment. "There's a big difference between someone following me into an alley and someone wanting to kill me."

"Think about it." He paused for a moment. "You saw Edwin Zachary with a woman who is a call girl. If that wasn't bad enough, she leaves her appointment book in your car and that book not only contains the initials and sexual preferences of her clients, but also contains the phone number of the woman responsible for running an exclusive sex ring."

"But how would anyone know that?"

She was so naive that Rafe couldn't help but give her a quizzical smile. "Sara, you *called* her. You gave her your name. If the Feds really were tapping her phone, it wouldn't take long for them to figure out who you are. Within five minutes of you revealing your identity, there wouldn't be an aspect of your life that the Feds didn't know about."

Sara waved her hand for him to stop. "Yes, I get all that. But why would the Feds want to kill me? I have nothing to do with the Glass Slipper Club."

"I'm not saying it's the Feds, but if anyone has the means to kill you, someone in Zachary's position would. You're a journalist, Sara, and he knows that. There's no telling what he might be willing to do to keep you from exposing his involvement with this club."

Slowly, Sara leaned forward and covered her face with her hands. "I don't believe this," she breathed. "I felt someone watching me while I was waiting for you back at the café. But the man I thought was staring at me turned out to be a father waiting for his wife and child."

Rafe's lips compressed in sympathy. "These men

didn't want you to notice them. From the way they moved and communicated, I'd say they have some military background."

"But why do they feel they have to kill me? Why don't they just warn me off?"

"At a guess, I'd say they want to keep you from sharing whatever information you have."

Her gaze shot to him in alarm. "What do you mean? What information? Why would they think I have any information beyond what they might have overheard during my telephone conversation with Juliet?"

Rafe sharpened his gaze on her, instinct telling him that she was hiding something.

"You write for a popular magazine," he said, carefully. "You have Colette's date book. Even if you can't prove who her clients were, you happened to see something the other night that could incriminate Edwin Zachary and perhaps even cost him his bid for the presidency. At the very least, if you decide to share your story with the world, people will begin asking questions and his reputation would undoubtedly suffer. Perhaps he wants to avoid that. At any cost."

Dropping her hands, Sara stared at him in disbelief. "I don't stand a chance, then. I mean, what do I know about evading someone with that kind of experience?" She gave a bitter laugh. "They probably know where I am right now. I'll be dead by morning."

She was so obviously freaked out, that Rafe decided not to tell her about the shorn bolts on her balcony. Sometimes, ignorance really was bliss. He would just need to be extra vigilant and make sure that she didn't do anything or go anywhere without him. But first he needed to gain her trust and make her feel safe.

"That's why I brought you here," he said, returning to sit beside her on the sofa, although he was careful to keep some distance between them. "Nobody is going to harm you, Sara."

Sara looked at him, and, although her face was pale, a ghost of a smile touched her lips. "You're just one man. Even with your background, what can you do if someone as powerful as Edwin Zachary wants to get rid of me?"

He allowed himself a smug smile. "You'd be surprised." Seeing her uncertainty, he sobered. "You'll have to trust me. I will protect you, even with my body if necessary."

"Why?" she asked. "Why are you doing this for me? You don't even know me. I'm pretty sure you don't even like me very much."

Rafe couldn't tell her why he viewed journalists with suspicion without admitting to his role in the rescue of the aid workers. "Let's just say I have a mistrust of journalists." He let his gaze drift deliberately over her features. "Especially pretty ones. As long as you're not trying to interview me, I like you just fine."

He watched as color seeped back into her face and she reached blindly for her beer, taking a hefty swig before setting the bottle back down with a thump.

"Well, don't forget those men saw you, too. They saw you sitting with me at the café and they saw you kiss me. They probably already know who you are. Maybe they think we're romantically involved." She cast a wild look around his townhouse. "What if they've already surrounded the place, and are just waiting to make their move?"

Rafe frowned, realizing she was teetering on the edge of a full-blown panic attack. Moving quickly, he crouched in front of her and took her hands in his. Her fingers were cold, and he rubbed them between his hands. “Hey,” he said quietly. “Look at me.”

She did, her eyes dark with whatever imagined horrors were going through her head.

“Nothing is going to happen. If they’ve figured out who I am, then they know better than to come after me. Especially in my own home.”

“What if we go to the police?” she asked hopefully, ignoring his words. “They could help us.”

“If their intent really is to kill you, then you’d be dead before you reached the station,” Rafe replied flatly. “And our only proof is initials in a book. Our best bet right now is to stick together and figure out a way to make you more valuable to them alive. But nothing is going to happen to you while I’m here. Okay?”

Sara nodded and dropped her gaze to where he still held her hands. She’d relaxed fractionally and when she spoke, her voice had lost some of its tight anxiety.

“Okay. But I still don’t understand why you’re doing this. I’m not your responsibility and I’m sure you have better things to do than act as my bodyguard, especially considering you’re supposed to be on leave right now. You know, rest and relaxation?”

Up close, he could see her eyes weren’t a pure blue, but a mixture of blues and grays, ringed in black and startlingly vivid in her pale face. Aside from her mouth, they had been the first thing he’d noticed about her. Rafe thought he could easily spend hours staring at her eyes, and wondered how many other men had fallen under their spell. Sara seemed to have little idea of just how stunning she was. She wore almost no cosmetics and did nothing to draw attention to her unusual features, or her curvy figure. In fact, she seemed out of place in a city as sophisticated as Washington, D.C..

Then Rafe remembered Ann Lonquist had been sweet and pretty, too. Or so he'd thought. She'd completely duped him with her damsel-in-distress act, and, while Sara Sinclair might not bear a strong physical resemblance to Ann, there was no denying the similarities between the two women. Dragging his gaze from her, he stood up and turned away, rubbing a hand across the back of his neck. He'd made a mistake in getting involved with Sara, but he'd never been able to walk away from an unfair fight, and there was no way Sara could handle this particular battle on her own. Whether he liked it or not, he was committed to seeing this through to the end.

"I'm not doing this for you," he finally responded, knowing he was lying through his teeth. "Let's just say this is what I consider rest and relaxation."

8

LONG AFTER SARA HAD SAID good-night to Rafe, she lay awake in his guest room, unable to stop thinking about the events of the day. She still had a difficult time believing that anyone would want to harm her because of what she had witnessed, but deep inside, she knew it was true. There had been something in Rafe's eyes when he'd told her about the men who had followed her that had left her in no doubt as to the sincerity of his words. Even if Rafe hadn't told her about his suspicions, her own gut instinct had told her the same thing.

Curling on her side, she bunched the pillow beneath her head and listened to the unfamiliar sounds of Rafe's townhouse. A clock ticked very quietly in the guestroom, and she could hear the soft whir of his dishwasher downstairs. She'd left her bedroom door open just a crack and a bar of light from the hallway fell across the floor. She knew that Rafe was just across the hall; she'd lain motionless as he'd come up the stairs and gone into his own room. Part of her had wondered if he would stop by her door or maybe come into her bedroom, and how she would react if he did. But his footsteps hadn't paused or even slowed in front of her room.

Just remembering the heated intensity of his kiss and the scrape of his callused hands across her bare skin and she was aroused all over again. She knew now that Rafe was attracted to her, but he probably had some innate sense of honor that would prevent him from acting on his desires. He was probably old-fashioned enough to believe that would be taking unfair advantage of her, when he'd claimed that she would be safe with him.

She should be grateful that he had enough respect for her not to expect her to sleep with him in return for saving her life. Of course, he was gorgeous enough that he probably had women throwing themselves at him without having to do a thing. With a groan, Sara rolled onto her back, feeling tight and uncomfortable in her own skin. The truth was, if she was even a little more assertive or confident, she'd be one of those women.

How would he react if she walked across the hallway to his room, and asked if she could stay with him? If she stepped out of her own comfort zone and became the aggressor? Would he turn her around and gently send her back to her own bed, or would his eyes flare with hunger as he drew her into his arms?

Just the thought of having sex with Rafe—of having his hard, male body inside her own—caused heat to swamp her limbs. Her breasts ached and she shifted restlessly beneath the sheet. She couldn't recall the last time she'd experienced such intense *need*. Everything about him turned her on, from the expression in his coffee-dark eyes when he looked at her to the strength and grace of his body. She recalled the few times he'd actually smiled and how that brief flash of humor had transformed his face. Even his voice was sexy, with its low, rasping quality. Most of all, she liked how he made her feel—fragile and feminine.

Safe.

Sexy.

Turning onto her stomach, she bent her arms under the pillow and stared at the small clock on the bedside table. Almost midnight. She'd come to bed more than two hours ago, and yet sleep eluded her. She tried closing her eyes, but even through her closed lids she imagined she could see the light slanting in from the hallway.

Pushing the blankets back, Sara sat up and swung her legs to the floor. Maybe if she turned the hallway light off, she could finally fall asleep. Her usual nightwear consisted of a camisole top and her underwear, but in deference to Rafe, she'd also packed flannel lounge pants. They rode low on her hips as she made her way cautiously to her door and peeked out.

Rafe's bedroom was diagonally across the hall from her own and she could see he'd left his door open just a crack. His room was dark. There was a light switch directly next to Rafe's door. If she was very quiet, she could hit the switch and be back in bed without him even knowing.

Slowly, she pushed her door open and stepped into the hall, wincing as a floorboard creaked ever so slightly beneath her weight. With careful deliberation, her arms outstretched for balance, she made her way across the hallway and actually had her fingers on the light switch, when Rafe's door swung open, startling a scream from her.

"Ohmigod," she gasped, doubling over in relief. "You scared me!"

"What are you doing?" He frowned at her from the open doorway, one arm braced on the door frame as he swept his midnight gaze over her, missing nothing.

Sara straightened and pushed her hair back from her face. "I couldn't sleep," she explained in a rush, "and the light was shining into my room, so I thought if I turned it off..."

Her voice trailed away as she realized that Rafe wore nothing but a pair of stretchy boxer briefs. She couldn't help but stare at him. He had powerful shoulders and a chest that could have been chiseled out of rock. His stomach was ridged with muscle, and the cotton briefs hugged his lean hips and emphasized his strong thighs. Everywhere she looked, his smooth skin was the color of warm honey, and she had to curl her fingers into her palms to keep from touching him.

"Sorry," he said, seemingly unaware that her mouth had gone dry and that she couldn't breathe or even form a single coherent thought. "I thought you'd be more comfortable if I kept the hall light on."

"I...I don't like the lights on," she finally managed, her voice coming out as a breathless croak.

His mouth lifted in a lazy smile. "In my experience, not many women do."

Sara blinked at him. Did he mean...? Oh, Lord, he did. And suddenly, vivid images of herself, stretched naked across his bed with the lights on while he looked his fill, swamped her imagination. Immediately, her earlier hunger returned, uncoiling and stretching until even her fingertips ached for him. As she stood immobile, his gaze drifted downward, stopping briefly at her mouth before descending to her breasts, and then lower to where she knew her navel and hipbones were exposed by the low-riding flannel pants.

Her breathing hitched when she saw the heat that flared in his eyes. He went very still and a muscle worked in his lean jaw, and, even as Sara watched, his body stirred beneath the stretchy boxers.

"Go to bed, Sara," he said, his voice a low rasp. "It's late."

"Almost midnight," she agreed. Her heart rate accelerated and her breathing quickened, as if she'd run up a flight of stairs. What was it she'd said to herself about stepping out of her comfort zone? Did she dare do it? More importantly, could she live with the consequences, whatever those might be? He might reject her. Then again, he might not. She took a steadying breath. "My mother always said nothing good ever happens after midnight."

"Your mother would be right."

Hardly aware of moving, Sara took a step toward him. He stood back and opened the door fractionally wider. It was all the invitation Sara needed. She'd never done anything so bold in her entire life as reaching out and laying her palm against the firm muscles of his chest. Beneath her fingers, she could feel the hard thump of his heart. Sara raised her gaze to his.

"I think she was wrong," she murmured.

RAFE HAD BEEN A GONER the moment he'd opened his door and seen Sara standing there. She was wearing a stretchy camisole top that emphasized the lush fullness of her breasts and exposed her midriff. More than anything, he wanted to explore that smooth stretch of pale skin, to feel again the silken texture of her stomach and explore her feminine curves.

He'd tried to do the right thing and send her back to her room. But the moment she'd taken a step toward him, he'd lost any ability to resist her. Her coppery hair was tousled around her face and her eyes had turned dark, the pupils dilated so that they nearly consumed her irises. Her mouth was soft and lush and when she touched him, he found himself stepping back and silently inviting her in.

She came willingly into his arms, her hands sliding over his bare shoulders to curl around the nape of his neck and draw his head down to hers. Everywhere she touched him, his skin burned. Rafe wasn't shy around women, but her directness momentarily stunned him. He hadn't been able to get her out of his head, but one of the reasons he hadn't pushed her for more downstairs, on the couch, was because he'd truly believed she didn't have that much experience with men. He hadn't wanted to scare her off, so he'd pulled back. But it seemed he'd been wrong about her.

Her mouth touched his and for a fraction of an instant, he stood frozen. He shouldn't get involved with her; he knew that. She was too tempting. Too irresistible. And that made her dangerous. Especially to a man whose career guaranteed that he wouldn't be around much.

But then she began to move her soft lips against his, and the sensation was so luxurious that he gave a groan of surrender and brought his arms around her, crushing her against his chest. She made a sound of pleasure in her throat and pressed closer, spearing her fingers through his hair and using her tongue to press past his lips and tentatively touch his. Pure lust jackknifed through Rafe, and without breaking the kiss, he bent and scooped her fully into his arms, kicking the door shut before carrying her over to his bed.

Bending one knee on the mattress, he laid her down and then followed her with the length of his body. She clung to him, her arms wound around his neck as she stretched sensuously beneath him. The street lamps cast muted light through the bedroom windows, bathing her in silver.

"God," he muttered against her mouth, "you drive me crazy."

He felt her smile, and took the opportunity to deepen the kiss and explore the damp silk of her mouth. He captured her soft moan, fusing their lips together as she held his head in her hands.

With supreme effort, he dragged his mouth from hers and bit a tender path along her jaw to where her heart pulsed erratically against the base of her throat. She gasped and arched upward, and slid one hand to the small of his back to urge him closer. Bracing his weight on one forearm, he lifted himself away from her enough to grasp the hem of her camisole and drag it upward. She helped him, pulling it over her head until she was gloriously bare beneath him.

"Jesus," he muttered, cupping his hand around one breast. "You're the prettiest thing I've seen in a long time."

He bent his head and flicked the dusky nipple with his tongue. Her breathing hitched and her hips shifted restlessly beneath him. Skating his hand along her ribs, he stroked the curve of her hip until he encountered the waistband of her soft flannel pants and slid his fingers beneath the fabric.

"Take these off," he demanded, his voice low and rough with need.

"Yes," she breathed, and lifted her hips to help him as he pushed the material down and then kicked them free.

She wore nothing beneath the soft pants, and Rafe sucked in his breath at the sight of her pale skin and the shadow of soft curls at the juncture of her thighs. Her breasts rose and fell rapidly, and when he stroked the back of his knuckles across her stomach, her muscles contracted.

"Are you sure about this?" he growled softly.

For a moment, she didn't respond and he had an instant of panic. Once they slept together, everything would change. He knew enough about himself to know that keeping her safe would become personal. She wasn't like the usual women that he hooked up with during his brief periods at home. Those women were only looking for physical pleasure; they weren't interested in a relationship and they definitely weren't interested in waiting for him while he deployed. But instinct told him that Sara was altogether different, and that scared the hell out of him.

But right now, with her sprawled sweetly beneath him, his own arousal was such that he pushed his misgivings aside. He wanted her. Badly. He'd just have to hope that she didn't get attached to him. Maybe he was wrong—maybe she only wanted the pleasure he could give her. Maybe she wouldn't want more than he could give. He'd been wrong about her on other things; why not on this, too?

"I'm sure," she finally said, and she reached down and cupped him through his briefs.

The sensation of her hand on his rigid cock caused him to groan, and he bent his head once more and caught her mouth with his own. She was incredibly responsive, arching against him and sliding her lips against his so that pleasure lashed through him. She stroked him through the fabric of his boxers, before easing her hand beneath the waistband to grasp him in her fingers. Her touch was like an electric shock, and he jerked reflexively in her hand.

"You're so hard," she murmured against his mouth, rubbing one finger across the head of his erection, "and hot."

Oh, yeah.

He eased himself to his side to give her better access to his body, holding her in the curve of his arm as he used his free hand to explore her more fully. She turned in to him, and he ran his hand along the curve of her waist and over her hip before cupping her buttock, enjoying the satiny softness of her skin. But when he dipped his fingers between her cheeks and teased her intimately from behind, she gave a cry of surprise and jerked against him.

"Shh," he soothed, stroking her softness. "Let me."

She made an incoherent sound and buried her face against his neck, pressing damp kisses against his throat, even as her hand continued to explore him. He was stiff and aching and wanted nothing more than to turn her on her back, spread her thighs and thrust himself into her, but he forced himself to slow down. He separated her feminine folds with his fingers, finding her slick with moisture.

"Ah, sweetheart," he groaned, "you're already wet." Slowly, he eased one finger into her, feeling her inner muscles contract around him even as she closed her hand around his cock. She was incredibly tight, and his balls ached with the need for release.

She withdrew her hand from his body and wordlessly pushed his boxers down until he could shimmy them free. Then there was nothing between them.

Rafe hooked a hand behind her knee and drew her leg across his hip, opening her for him as he resumed stroking her, swirling moisture over the small rise of flesh until she made an inarticulate sound of pleasure and shivered in his arms.

"Good?" he murmured against her ear, before tracing the delicate lobe with his tongue.

"Oh, yeah," she breathed.

He was positioned at the entrance to her body and it would take no more than one small movement to nudge his way inside, but it was suddenly important to him that Sara want him as much as he wanted her. Easing two fingers into her, he thrust them slowly in and out, and then caught her mouth with his own, using his tongue to imitate the movement of his hand. She groaned deeply.

Pushing her onto her back, Rafe came over her and began working his way down the length of her body with his mouth, while continuing to torment her with his fingers. She watched him through hazy eyes, her lower lip caught between her teeth. He licked her breasts, suckling first one nipple and then the other before moving lower, skating his tongue along her smooth stomach while his fingers worked strongly inside her. Her hips lifted into his hand, and when he reached her navel, he dipped his tongue inside before dragging his lips away to kiss the inside of one thigh. Then, as he continued to stroke her, he bent his head and touched his tongue to her clitoris. She gave a strangled cry and her hips bucked, but Rafe had no mercy. He continued to lave her with soft laps, while his fingers caressed her until she cried out and her whole body convulsed. Rafe felt her muscles contracting around his fingers, but he didn't stop until he'd wrung every last shudder from her and she collapsed weakly against the pillow.

Only then did he come completely over her, using his knee to spread her thighs. He was completely jacked, but he still had enough sense to reach over and jerk open the drawer of his bedside table and pull out an unopened box of condoms. Watching her come apart had been a complete turn-on and he couldn't remember the last time he'd been this hard for a woman. With hands that weren't quite steady, he ripped the box open and peeled a condom from a foil packet.

"Okay?" he asked, his voice rough with need.

She gave a shaky laugh and drew him down. "I don't know," she confessed. "Am I still alive?"

"Oh, yeah," he breathed, and covered himself. "Let me show you."

SARA HAD NEVER EXPERIENCED an orgasm like the one Rafe Delgado had just given her. Heck, she'd never experienced a man like Rafe in her entire life. The reality of being with him eclipsed anything she had ever imagined. She'd thought she knew what it was like to be in a physical relationship, but Rafe had shattered those notions in less than fifteen minutes. What had taken her weeks to do in previous relationships, he'd coaxed from her in less than fifteen minutes.

A part of her thought she should feel some shame at having given him so much so soon, but another part of her wanted to give him even more. She wanted to give him everything, and take as much in return.

Her body still thrummed with sexual satisfaction as Rafe came over her and even in the indistinct light, she could see the tautness of his expression. With his black eyes and slashing brows, and the unyielding thrust of his jaw, there was something almost dangerous about him. He used his legs to nudge her own farther apart, and then there he was, hot and hard against her center, where she still throbbed from her orgasm. She held her breath as he pushed one of her knees wider, and then slowly surged forward, stretching and filling her.

Sara gasped and clung to his shoulders as he settled himself fully inside her. She flexed her inner muscles around his rigid length, and sucked in her breath as he ground closer, rubbing himself against her sensitized flesh.

"Oh, man," he groaned, "that feels too good."

Sara agreed. Nothing had ever felt as pleasurable as Rafe's body moving inside her own. Even now, while she was sated and weak-limbed from her orgasm, she could feel tension coiling tightly where they were joined.

Dim light slanted in through his window, casting his features in partial shadow and emphasizing the hard angles of his cheekbones. He withdrew from her body and then sank back into her in a series of bone-melting thrusts that had her drawing her knees further back and hooking her heels into the small of his back.

He braced his weight on either side of her and bent his head to press a searing kiss across her mouth. Sara responded hungrily, tightening her thighs around his hips as she clutched at his shoulders. Rafe's breathing grew harsh and his movements became more urgent. He thrust harder into her, until heat gathered where he stroked her and she could feel the beginnings of another orgasm building.

"I want you to come again." Rafe's voice was a low, sensual growl. He punctuated his command with another slow, deep thrust that caused Sara to give a breathless cry of startled pleasure.

Rafe's hips moved faster and he bent his head to her shoulder, one hand slipping beneath her to grasp her buttock and urge her closer. He was everywhere; surrounding her and inside her, his breath mingling with hers and his heart pounding hard against her own. His skin was damp with sweat and his powerful muscles bunched with effort as he pumped into her.

"I can't— I have to—" With a hoarse cry, Rafe drove into her one last time, and the raw need in his voice was enough to push Sara over the edge, as well. She arched upward, holding on to him for dear life as she fractured around him in a white-hot explosion of pleasure.

Several long moments passed as she lay beneath him, stunned and shaken. His heavy weight pinned her to the bed and she hugged him closer, savoring the feel of him. He turned his face and pressed his lips against her neck. Sara smiled. So this is what came of being assertive. It seemed her mother had been wrong, after all.

Some of the best things happened after midnight.

9

Sara woke to the smell of freshly brewed coffee and the warmth of sunlight on her face. Opening her eyes, she lay disoriented for a moment, not recognizing her surroundings. Then she remembered.

Rafe, making love to her. Not just once, but twice. They'd fallen asleep after the first time, but she'd woken up just before dawn to the feel of him pressed warmly against her back and his hands slowly exploring her. She still couldn't believe how quickly he'd aroused her. This time, he'd taken her from behind while she'd lain on her side, stroking her with his fingers as he'd filled her and pushed her over the edge. She had fallen back to sleep with him still inside her.

Sitting up, she realized she was still nude, and she dragged the sheet up to her neck. She needn't have bothered. She was alone in Rafe's bedroom. The blankets were rumpled and the pillow next to her still bore the imprint of his head. The door to the adjoining bathroom was open. He must have showered while she slept, because she could smell the soap that she was coming to associate with him.

She hadn't gotten a good look at his room during the night, and now she glanced around with interest. His tastes were conservative and practical, and there was nothing out of place. No dirty laundry on the floor, even her flannel pajama bottoms and camisole had been laid across the foot of the bed. A stack of neatly folded shirts, still wrapped in protective plastic with a dry-cleaning tag attached, sat on his dresser next to several framed photos.

Dragging the sheet around her, Sara slipped from the bed and went to inspect. The first was of Rafe and an older woman. Judging from the resemblance, the woman had to be his mother. The second photo showed Rafe and three other men, all in their military dress blues.

Turning from the dresser, Sara opened the double doors of an enormous closet. Inside, Rafe's uniforms hung side by side with civilian clothing and he had at least six pairs of military boots lined up on the floor. Next to these were several pairs of dress shoes that were polished to such a high sheen, Sara was certain she could have done her makeup in her reflection from them. Two duffel bags were stashed toward the back of the closet and judging from their size, they were packed and ready to go at a moment's notice.

Sort of like Rafe.

"Looking for something?"

Startled, Sara turned to see Rafe leaning in the doorway of the bedroom, a steaming mug of coffee in one hand. He watched her closely, and although she couldn't detect any censure in his expression, he wasn't exactly smiling at her, either.

"Sorry," she murmured, closing the closet doors and clutching the sheet to her. "I was just being nosey."

He came into the room and handed her the mug, and a ghost of a smile touched his mouth as he studied her. He wore a pair of jeans and a black shirt that gave him a slightly menacing appearance. She was acutely conscious of her own nudity.

"It's fine," he assured her. "I've been known to be nosey myself, on occasion."

She knew it was an indirect apology for having gone through her purse and gave him a quick nod. Despite what they had shared during the night, he seemed remote and cool. A stranger. She didn't know what to say or how to act, and bent her face over her coffee mug to hide her confusion.

"I'll let you get showered and dressed," he finally said. "Then we should probably talk."

Slowly, Sara raised her gaze to meet his. His expression was unfathomable and she found it hard to believe he was the same man who, just hours earlier, had touched her so intimately. She nodded mutely and watched as he left, scrubbing a hand across the back of his neck as he went.

After he was gone, she sat down on the edge of the bed, feeling bereft. Worse, she felt used. Rafe certainly hadn't distanced himself from her during the night, but it seemed he couldn't bring himself even to kiss her this morning. He'd probably been grateful that she'd still been asleep when he'd woken up, affording him the opportunity to escape.

Was this what a one-night stand felt like? If so, Sara decided this would be her one and only. She gave a huff of laughter. She'd been so determined to step out of her comfort zone and do something assertive, and the result was that she felt worse than ever.

RAFE WAS LEANING AGAINST the kitchen island scanning a newspaper and drinking his coffee when she finally came downstairs. He straightened when she came into the kitchen, his dark gaze sliding over her, and she knew he took in every detail of her appearance. She wore a pair of jeans and a black cashmere sweater that hugged her curves. She'd figured if he could wear black, then so could she. It was fitting actually.

"Hey," she murmured, placing her empty mug in the sink.

"Sara—"

"I know what you're going to say," she interrupted. Drawing a deep breath, she turned toward him and braced her hands on the sink behind her. Bracing herself.

He merely raised one eyebrow and waited.

Sara felt herself flushing but pushed determinedly on. "You're going to say that last night was a mistake. You're going to tell me that you're not able to get into any kind of relationship right now, and you're afraid that I might read more into what happened than what was there. Right?"

He frowned. "No, damn it. That isn't what I was going to say." Pushing away from the counter, he came around the island and stood in front of her, crowding her. "I was going to say that after last night, I don't think I'm the best person to protect you from whoever is after you. I was going to say that because of last night, I can't be objective about you."

"Oh." Sara blinked at him. "So…last night wasn't a mistake?"

To her surprise, he laughed softly and slid a hand beneath her hair. "Oh, no, lady. I didn't say that. Last night was definitely a mistake—a freaking huge mistake that I'd repeat in a heartbeat."

"Oh." She searched his eyes, seeing that he was completely serious. Last night had meant something to him. Enough that he was admitting that she'd compromised his objectivity. "I thought—this morning—"

"I know," he said, his voice husky. "But if I'd done what I wanted to do this morning, we'd still be in that bed."

"You say that like it's a bad thing." She smiled, feeling the hard knot in her chest begin to loosen.

His hand massaged the nape of her neck. "I meant what I said, Sara. I can't protect you if I'm emotionally involved."

Emotionally involved.

Sara felt her heart thump hard. Was it possible that after just one night this hard man could really have feelings for her?

"So what are you suggesting?"

He dropped his hand. "I have a friend who lives in North Carolina with his wife. He's Special Ops. You could stay with them for a week or so, until we get this figured out."

Sara looked at him in disbelief. "You're kidding."

"I'm dead serious."

Sara pushed away from the sink and put both hands up to forestall him. "Okay, let's get one thing straight. I am not going to North Carolina to stay with complete strangers. You were the one who suggested I stay with you for a week and I'm willing to do that. But there's no way I'm going to North Carolina."

"It wasn't a request," he said drily.

Sara drew in a deep breath and tipped her chin up. "If I can't stay here with you, then I'm returning to my own apartment." Rafe's expression was dark enough that her stomach twisted with nerves. "I'm not going to North Carolina, and that's final."

"Sara—"

"I can help you find out who was following me," she insisted. "Rafe, this is my life we're talking about. Please, let me help you."

He turned away and raked a hand over his short hair, clearly unconvinced. But at least he wasn't giving her an unequivocal refusal. Emboldened, she reached out and laid a hand on his arm, feeling the steely muscles that corded his forearm.

"We're not even sure these men are still after me," she reasoned. "We don't know for sure what they wanted yesterday when they followed me into the alley. We could be completely overreacting."

His mouth tightened and he looked down at her hand on his arm. He looked as if he were debating with himself, and then finally he gave her a curt nod. "Okay. You'll stay with me. But if at any time I think it's too dangerous for you to continue to stay here, you'll go to North Carolina. No arguments."

"Rafe—" She started to protest.

"I'm not willing to compromise on this, Sara. Not when it comes to your safety." His tone was unyielding. "You need to trust me on this."

Sara nodded, recognizing that he was serious and relieved that he was willing to let her stay. She didn't want to go back to her apartment. The thought of being there by herself after having spent the past hours with Rafe held no appeal. She especially didn't relish the thought of being alone at night in her apartment. Even if Rafe decided they shouldn't sleep together again, she'd rather be here than there.

"Okay," she agreed. "I'll trust you."

He gave her a slow smile that transformed his face. "Good. Now about last night…don't you know it's dangerous to creep around a man's house wearing next to nothing, when he's lying in bed fantasizing about you?"

Sara felt herself blushing as he cupped her face in his hands and lowered his head to press a warm kiss against her mouth. She couldn't help but respond, curling her fingers around the muscles of his arms and leaning into him. Too soon, he lifted his head.

His expression was rueful as he considered her. "I knew from the moment I saw you at the ball that you were trouble."

"And yet you still agreed to meet with me," she said, smiling.

He laughed. "Yeah. Little did I know that my training and background were no match for the weapons that you have at your disposal." Then, as if he'd said too much, he turned away and opened the fridge and peered inside. "Hungry? I make a mean omelet."

SARA SAT NEXT TO RAFE on his sofa, the little planner open in her hands. They'd spent the past hour poring over the entries and trying to decipher the initials of the clients. Together, they'd drawn up a list of the male cabinet members in the White House, as well as those in Congress and the Senate. Rafe had a laptop across his thighs and was compiling a list of high-ranking military men, as well.

"Although, I wonder if we ought not to include females, too," mused Sara.

"I did some checking," Rafe said absently. "The Glass Slipper Club only caters to male clientele."

"You did some checking?" Sara stared at him. "How? The club has been shut down."

He slanted her a tolerant look.

"Okay," Sara relented. "I get it. You're covert operations. There isn't anything you don't know or can't find out. Do I have it right?"

He flashed her a grin. "Pretty much."

Sara leaned over and glanced at the list he was building. "Holy smokes. That's a lot of names." She checked her list of initials. "Some of these initials are so common that they could belong to anybody on that list. Or not on that list, for that matter."

"Yes, but you also have some unusual combinations that shouldn't be too difficult to match." Leaning sideways so that his shoulder touched hers, he indicated a set of initials. "Take this one, for example. How many people could possibly have the initials W.W.?"

Sara frowned. "Those could belong to William Worthington, I suppose, although I can't really picture him involved in something like this. Maybe they belong to Wes Wight," she suggested, naming a popular political commentator.

"Read me an entry for W.W.," Rafe suggested.

Sara thumbed through the pages of the planner until she found one. "Okay, here's one: 'W.W.—Dominant alpha. Likes bondage and rough play. Bring blindfold and silk stockings.'"

"My bet is on Worthington," he said drily.

Sara made a face. "*Ew.* Why would you think that?"

Rafe shrugged. "Look at the guy."

"Yeah, that's what I mean. He's a nasty little worm of a man."

Rafe returned his attention to the laptop. "Exactly. He's probably dominated by his wife, or maybe he feels worthless as a man. The Glass Slipper Club lets him play out his fantasies and let's face it…" He cast her a roguish grin. "Who doesn't fantasize about blindfolds and silk stockings?"

Sara's breath caught at the wicked gleam in his dark eyes. She could picture it clearly—Rafe, bound naked to the bed with a blindfold over his eyes, while she tormented him with her hands and mouth.

"Yes," she breathed. "I see what you mean."

His gaze sharpened on her with interest. "Do you?"

Swallowing hard, Sara dragged her gaze from his and flipped through the planner again. "What about this one? 'J.F.—Playful. Fun. Bring all the toys. Nothing too wild.'" She frowned. "I wonder if she meant that she shouldn't bring anything too wild, or that nothing *is* too wild for J.F.?"

Rafe set the laptop aside and turned toward her on the sofa. A secretive smile lifted up the corners of his mouth as he watched her. "I'd say nothing is too wild. Bring it on, he's game for anything."

Sara tipped her head as she considered Rafe. "Now why would you guess that? Do you know this J.F.?"

Slowly, Rafe reached out and caught her around the waist and dragged her toward him until she was half lying across his lap. "No," he murmured, studying her mouth, "but that's what I would mean. Nothing would be too wild."

"Ah." Sara let her gaze drift over his face, taking in the color that rode high on his sculpted cheekbones and the languorous expression in his eyes. "What would Colette have written about you, I wonder, if you were a Glass Slipper client?"

"First of all," he breathed in a husky tone, bending his head to nip playfully at her neck, "you'd never find my name on any client list. Paying for sex is not my idea of a good time."

Sara laughed breathlessly and tipped her head to the side to allow him better access. She gasped as his tongue found the sensitive area behind her ear and had to struggle to focus. "Well then, what fantasy would you like to see fulfilled? Maybe I'll add my own entry."

Holding her in the crook of his arm, he slipped his free hand beneath her sweater, his warm palm smoothing over her ribcage until he cupped her breast. Sara sucked in a breath as he began to caress her nipple through the lace bra she wore.

"This is my fantasy," he growled softly, pulling the bra down and her sweater up until her breasts were exposed to his gaze. "Having hot sex with a dangerous woman. Or dangerous sex with a hot woman."

He fondled one breast, and bent his head to draw the other one into his mouth, suckling and nibbling on her aroused nipple until she squirmed in his lap and pushed his head away.

"Oh, stop," she panted. "It's too much."

He lifted his head, but kept his hand over her breast, gently kneading and tormenting her. "Tell me what your fantasy would be," he urged.

This *was* her fantasy. *He* was her fantasy. She'd fantasized about him from the first night she'd met him, but she'd never actually believed they might be together like this.

"C'mon," he coaxed. "Tell me what you want."

Well…there had been one entry in the planner that had intrigued her. She risked a peek at Rafe's face, wondering if she should tell him. Wondering how he would react if she did. He watched her intently.

"Tell me," he urged, and slanted his mouth softly across hers—a moist, sensual fusing of their lips that caused spirals of heat to lick their way across her skin. She moaned and pressed herself into his hand.

Finally, she dragged her mouth free, breathing heavily. "Okay," she said against his lips. "But promise you won't laugh."

He kissed her again, deeply. "I promise. Now tell me."

"Come here." She drew his head down and whispered in his ear. As he drew back, his expression was one of raw, male need.

"*That's* your fantasy?"

"Well, one of them anyway." Sara knew her face was flaming. She couldn't believe she'd had the courage to tell him. But from the heated expression in his eyes, she knew she hadn't made a mistake.

"Oh, man," he groaned, "you are killing me, lady."

Sara lay back in his arms, enjoying how he made her feel. Sexy. Powerful. The promise in his eyes made her breath catch.

"You don't have to do anything you're not comfortable with," she assured him with a slow smile, knowing there was no way he'd refuse her. Not if his body's reaction was any indication. She could feel him beneath her, hard and ready.

"Trust me," he said with a lazy smile. "There's nothing I wouldn't feel comfortable doing with you. And if it kills me, at least I'll die happy."

10

RAFE GLANCED OVER AT SARA, who sat beside him in the passenger seat of his car. They'd spent several unforgettable hours exploring their fantasies, first in his living room and then upstairs in his bed. If he didn't have other obligations, Rafe thought he could have happily spent the entire day in bed with Sara.

He smiled as he recalled her secret fantasy of being dominated, of being forced to submit to him as he ravished her. As female fantasies went, he knew hers wasn't all that uncommon, and he'd been prepared to back off immediately if she gave him any indication she was truly afraid.

But when he'd pushed her up against a wall and pinned her arms over her head, she hadn't been frightened. She'd been excited, and that had aroused him. And when he'd shoved his hand into her jeans to stroke her, she'd been more than ready. He'd been forceful, but he'd been careful with her. And he was grateful as hell that she'd trusted him to help her fulfill that particular fantasy. He cringed to think what a different kind of man might have done, given that sort of control. Just the thought of another guy doing any of those things with Sara caused a tight knot to form in his chest.

Looking at her now, Rafe had a difficult time believing she was the same woman who had blown his mind just a few short hours ago. Gone was the flushed, uninhibited lover. In her place was a quiet, conservative woman who concentrated on responding to the messages on her phone and studiously avoided meeting his eyes. She'd tamed her hair into a neat ponytail and had applied some makeup and jewelry. In her button-down blouse and slacks, paired with a thigh-length trench coat, she at least presented an image of a Washington professional.

On one level, he understood that she might be self-conscious about what they'd done together earlier, but on the other hand he would have thought the experience would make her feel closer to him.

"Hey." Reaching over, he scooped a loose tendril of her hair behind her ear. "You okay?"

She flicked a glance in his direction and nodded, but he saw how the tips of her ears turned red. The knowledge that she was embarrassed by what they had done was both endearing and infuriating.

"Today was amazing," he said quietly. "*You* were amazing."

She cast him a grateful smile and set her phone down on her lap. "Thanks. I, um, can't believe some of the things I let you do." She gave a self-conscious laugh and covered her face briefly with her hands before turning to him with a look of appeal. "Please tell me you weren't horrified."

In answer, Rafe pulled the car to an abrupt stop on the side of the road, uncaring of the other motorists who blared their horns at him as they passed. Thrusting the vehicle into Park, he unfastened his seat belt and leaned over to grasp her by the shoulders.

"Sara, I meant what I just said. You were amazing." He rubbed the back of his knuckles across her cheek. "You're the sexiest woman I've ever known and I feel like the luckiest son of a bitch on the planet that you asked me to share that fantasy with you."

She smiled at him, and Rafe felt something shift in his chest. "Really?"

"I never joke about something as serious as sex with a beautiful woman."

To his relief, she laughed and then leaned forward to press a soft kiss against his mouth.

"How do you always know just the right thing to say and do?" she asked, resting her forehead against his shoulder.

Rafe chuckled and enfolded her in his arms. "You just don't know me well enough, yet. Trust me, I put my foot in it more than I care to admit. Give me time—I'm sure I'll say something to irritate the hell out of you."

Even as he said the words, Rafe realized he did want more time with Sara. He wanted to give her the chance to get to know him better, even his faults, and his tendency to say whatever he thought and damn the consequences. He'd never have believed he was the type of guy who could fall for someone after just one night, but he knew he was in danger of falling hard for Sarah.

"We'll see," Sara said, clearly unconvinced. Pulling out of his arms, she rubbed her finger over his mouth. "Sorry. Lipstick."

As Rafe eased the car back onto the thruway, she

tucked her phone into her handbag. "So how often do you do this?"

He couldn't help but tease her. "What? Convince unsuspecting women to move in with me for a week and then take advantage of them?"

She laughed softly. "No, not that, although I hope I'm the only one you've done that to. I mean, how often do you visit the guys at the Walter Reed Medical Center?"

Rafe shrugged. "When I'm here, I try to get over to the hospital a couple of times a week. A lot of those guys don't have family in this part of the country, so they really appreciate visitors. And they need to know that they haven't been forgotten."

"What about you? Were you ever injured?"

"No. I've been lucky. My guys and I have had some close calls, but I'm grateful to say that we've never lost a team member."

"Thank goodness," Sara breathed.

"Here we are," he said, pulling into the entrance of the medical center. "You'll see some things here that you'll find disturbing, even upsetting. But the important thing is not to show pity for these guys, okay? They won't thank you for it."

She nodded. "Okay."

"By the same token," he added, turning into a vacant parking spot and shutting the engine off, "if you find yourself getting overwhelmed, just let me know and we'll leave. Got it?"

Sara drew in a deep breath and let it out slowly. "Got it." She gave him a resolute smile. "I'm ready."

FOR THE NEXT SEVERAL HOURS, Sara watched as Rafe moved from hospital room to hospital room, greeting the patients with fist bumps or handshakes. Many of the soldiers knew him by name, and prior to entering each room, Rafe would quietly indicate to her whether the patient was someone he had visited before, or a recent admission to the hospital. He made no distinction as to rank or branch of service, and if Sara hadn't known better, she would have believed that he was a close personal friend of each patient.

He paused outside one room and caught Sara by the arm to keep her from entering. "This next guy is a unique case. He's been here for a couple of months, and a bunch of us take turns visiting him to keep his spirits up."

As they entered the room, Sara saw a man sitting up in his hospital bed with an electronic reader in his hand. He looked up when he heard Rafe's footsteps, and his face creased into a grin. His head had been shaved and bore the evidence of extensive surgery, with scars criss-crossing his scalp. Beneath the blanket that covered him, Sara realized he was also missing a leg.

"Hey, Delgado," he said, extending a hand. "Good to see you, man!" He looked over at Sara. "Who's this you brought with you?"

Rafe drew Sara forward. "I want you to meet a good friend, Sara Sinclair. She's doing a story for *American Man* magazine, and I thought she might like to meet a real hero, in the flesh. Sara, this is Corporal Shay Riordan. He and another soldier used their bodies as shields to protect members of their unit when an insurgent on a motorcycle rode by and detonated a bomb."

Shay gave Rafe a disgruntled look. "Damn it, Delgado, I'm no hero. You would have done the same thing. Any one of my team would have done the same thing.

We just happened to see the son of a bitch first and realized what he was up to." He extended a hand to Sara. "I'm pleased to meet you, Ms. Sinclair."

"Sara," she murmured. "Call me Sara."

"How is Kim doing?" Rafe asked, indicating a photo on his bedside table.

Shay sighed and shifted restlessly. "She's doing good. Getting impatient, I suspect. I just wish I could be there with her." He looked at Sara. "My wife is expecting our first baby in about five weeks. I haven't seen her because her pregnancy is considered high-risk and she can't travel." He gave a short laugh. "So here we are, both confined to bed on opposite sides of the country."

"I'm so sorry you can't be together," Sara murmured.

Shay shrugged. "At least I'm alive, and I know I'll be home in time to see our baby born. Nothing else matters."

There was a momentary silence in the room as they considered his words.

"Hey, did I thank you yet for the laptop?" Shay asked.

Rafe shook his head. "When did it arrive?"

"A couple of days ago." Leaning over the side of his bed, he lifted a silver laptop from his bedside table and set it across his thighs. "The Semper Fi Fund got this for me," he said, glancing at Sara. "It has a built-in webcam and lets my wife and I Skype each other at least a couple of times each day. It's almost as good as being there. Here, I'll show you."

Sara watched as he opened an application and keyed in a code. After a moment, he looked up with a sheepish expression. "She's probably sleeping. She's not online, so she doesn't realize I'm trying to call."

"That's okay," Rafe said with a grin. "She probably

wouldn't want to see a bunch of strangers staring back at her, anyway."

"Nah, she knows all about you. I told her that you're like family."

Rafe was quiet for a moment, but Sara could see that the other man's words had moved him. "Thanks, bro," he finally said, taking the corporal's hand in a firm grip. "I appreciate that. How long before they send you home?"

"With luck, my prosthetic will be ready by the end of the week. I'll need a couple of weeks of therapy to get used to walking with it, and then I'll be on my way."

"That's terrific. I'll be by in a few days to check out the new leg, okay?"

Shay grinned. "Sounds good."

As they left the room, Sara risked a glance at Rafe. "He seems to be in good spirits."

Rafe nodded in satisfaction. "Yeah, he's come a long way since he first got here. The doctors didn't expect him to survive. He was in a coma for weeks, and they thought if he did pull through he'd have profound brain damage."

"He seems fine."

"He will be."

"So whose idea was it to get him the laptop?"

"The Semper Fi Fund provided one for him and one for his wife."

They were walking toward the entrance of the hospital, when a nurse called to them from a nearby nursing station.

"Sergeant Delgado," she enthused. She was a pretty woman with sleek dark hair and eyes that practically devoured him on the spot. She swept Sara with one swift glance and then turned her attention back to Rafe. "I'm sorry I missed you the other day, but the flowers you sent arrived."

Sara arched a questioning look at Rafe, but he just smiled easily at the other woman. "Great."

"So...when will you be back?"

Rafe took Sara's elbow and steered her past the woman, toward the exit. "In a couple of days. See you then."

"Bye."

Sara didn't look back, but she was sure that if she did, she'd see the woman preening in the corridor.

"You bought her flowers?" she asked in a low voice, trying hard not to sound jealous but knowing she failed.

Rafe gave her a tolerant look. "No. I sent flowers to a certain female private who is recovering from injuries and I thought they would cheer her up."

"Oh."

They left the hospital and Rafe didn't release her arm as they walked back to the car. Sara was acutely conscious of his strong fingers, and couldn't help but recall what his hands were capable of doing to her. When they reached his car, instead of opening her door, Rafe pushed her up against it, following with the hard length of his body.

"I've wanted to do this for the past three hours," he muttered, bracketing her face in his palms. Bending his head, he claimed her mouth in a kiss that was both primal and possessive. Sara sagged weakly against him as he pushed past her lips and mated his tongue to hers. The car door was cold and hard at her back, but Rafe's body was warm and muscled and strong. Sliding her hands inside his open jacket, Sara reveled in his heat and returned his kiss with an abandon that might have shocked her just two days ago. But Rafe had an ability to make her lose her composure with little more than a look.

Rafe pulled away first, stepping back from the car. "That'll do until I get you home," he said with a wicked grin, and handed her into the passenger seat.

Sara watched as he rounded the hood of the sports car and eased behind the wheel. Her heart was still thudding in her chest and her mouth felt slightly bruised from the force of his kiss. His words caused a riot of emotions to surge through her. Anticipation. Confusion. And apprehension, because Sara suspected that spending too much time in Rafe Delgado's company could be very dangerous to her heart.

They drove in silence as Sara thought about all the people they had visited that day, and what it meant to them to have someone like Rafe in their lives. If she hadn't already known about his involvement with the Semper Fi Fund, she would have had a tough time believing it. She had the sense that despite the fact he worked as part of a team, he was a little bit of a loner.

"You visit a lot of friends at the hospital," she finally said, breaking the silence. "So what about when you're home?"

"What do you mean?"

"Well, you said you're on leave for a couple of weeks, and I just wondered who visits you when you're home."

He gave her a knowing smile as he maneuvered his way through the streets. "Are you asking if I have a girlfriend?"

Sara started, appalled. "No! Of course not." She looked suspiciously at him. "Why? Do you?"

He laughed and shook his head, and Sara felt a wave of relief at his response. He didn't have a girlfriend. Realistically, she knew she didn't have any claim on this man—even she wasn't naive enough to think that one night of incredible sex meant anything—but after spending the afternoon with him and seeing the time and care he took with the injured soldiers, she realized she wanted to know him better. And yes, she had been jealous when the nurse had tried to flirt with him.

"Okay, well that's good. I mean, I can't imagine a girlfriend would approve of you inviting me—a complete stranger—to spend the week with you." Never mind the hot sex.

"Sara," he interrupted. "I don't have a girlfriend."

"Right." She drew in a deep breath and looked away, afraid he might see her immense relief. "What about family? Do you have any family in the area?"

"Actually, I don't. My mother lives in Vermont and I have a sister in New York, but nobody in the D.C. area. Unless you count my Marine Corps buddies. They're pretty much my family both here and when I'm deployed."

Sara looked at him in surprise. She'd assumed he was from the Virginia area. But if his mother lived in Vermont, there was a likelihood that he'd lived there, too. "Do you see your mother and sister very often?"

He shrugged. "I try to get up there when I can."

"Is that where you were raised? In Vermont?"

"Yeah. My mom was a single parent and she ran a little shop in downtown Burlington." He glanced over at her. "I can see why you chose journalism as a career. You ask a lot of questions. What about you? When I first met you, I thought you seemed out of place here. Was I wrong?"

Sara looked down at her hands. "No. I was raised in a small town in central Pennsylvania. My parents were horrified when I told them I was going to live in Washington, D.C." She gave a small laugh as she recalled her mother's reaction. "My mom doesn't trust cities. She's still convinced that I'll be taken advantage of in every way possible."

Rafe slanted her one dark, heated look. "Well, the day is still young," he said. "One can always hope."

11

Thirty minutes later they reached Rafe's house. As he pulled into his neighborhood, Sara didn't miss how he carefully scanned the surrounding streets and his property for any signs that they might have been followed. But after parking the car, he all but dragged her into the house, not even waiting to remove their jackets before he hauled her into his arms.

"Christ, you feel good," he growled against her throat, his hands smoothing over her body to cup her bottom and pull her against him. His mouth seared a trail along her neck before he took her earlobe between his teeth and bit gently, causing shivers of sensation to chase across Sara's skin.

"You're wearing too many layers," he complained, and began unbuttoning her jacket, pushing the heavy garment from her shoulders to fall to the floor behind her.

Sara laughed unsteadily, but was cut short as he crushed her mouth to his own, angling her head for better access. Her hand slid upward over his arm to the slope of his shoulder, admiring the flex of muscle beneath the supple leather of his jacket. He deepened the kiss, licking at the inside of her mouth even as he began working on the tiny buttons of her blouse.

A heaviness swamped her limbs, and she clutched him around the neck, leaning into him and returning his kiss with equal intensity. She was only vaguely aware of Rafe slipping one hand behind her back to unfasten her bra and push it down, before cool air wafted across her bare skin. Then he dragged his lips from hers and bent his head to draw one nipple into his warm, wet mouth. The combination of heat and moisture sent an electric current to her groin, where she was already damp with need.

"I need— I want—"

Rafe didn't finish his thought. Instead, he moved her backwards until her bottom came into contact with the oversized arm of the leather sofa. Leaning over her, Rafe continued to torment her breasts with his mouth, laving first one and then the other with his tongue while his free hand deftly worked the snap of her slacks.

"Take these off," he muttered against her skin.

Sara didn't have the will to protest, not when his black eyes were so intent and his mouth and hands worked magic on her body. She complied eagerly, kicking her shoes off and helping him work the material over her hips and down the length of her legs until she wore only her panties. Her shirt fell open beneath his hands as he straightened enough to rake his gaze over her.

Sara was only vaguely aware that she felt no self-consciousness. Instead, she felt incredibly sexy as he peeled his leather jacket off and let it fall next to hers on the floor. Boldly, she reached out, caught him by his belt and pulled him toward her. His breathing was ragged.

"Now you're the one with too many clothes on," she said. Her voice sounded husky, even to her own ears. She fumbled with his belt. "Take this off."

His hands covered hers and he helped her to undo the buckle before she pushed his fingers aside, dragging his zipper down and cupping him through the fabric of his boxers. He was hard and hot and pulsing against her palm and Sara felt an answering throb of need between her legs. Sliding her legs to either side of his thighs, she drew him closer, until he was pressed against her center.

"This is where I want you," she whispered, and emphasized her words with a soft grinding of her hips against his.

Rafe groaned and leaned over her, kissing her deeply as he eased her back so that she reclined at an angle with her hips up on the arm of the sofa.

Rafe straightened and withdrew his wallet from his back pocket. Sara saw his hands were a little unsteady as he pulled a condom out and tore it open with his teeth. Her mouth went dry as he released himself from his boxers and covered his erection.

"You're so damned gorgeous," he rasped. "I'm sorry, but I can't wait..."

"I don't want you to," Sara breathed, and watched in fascination as he swiftly drew her panties over her hips and down the length of her legs until she was gloriously bare. She found herself excited by the fact that while she was almost completely naked, he was still semi-clothed. She caught her breath as he deliberately drew his finger along her throbbing flesh.

"Oh," she gasped and raised her hips, silently inviting more of the delicious contact.

"Soon," he promised, parting her folds and using his thumb to swirl moisture over her clitoris. "You're so wet, so responsive."

"It's you," Sara said, panting. "You do this to me."

The sensation of his fingers against her aroused flesh was almost more than she could take, and she heard herself moan softly. As if he knew she couldn't hold on much longer, Rafe grasped her ankles and pushed her knees back and then wide, opening her to him.

"I'm sorry, sweetheart," he rasped, and nudged himself just inside the entrance to her body. "I can't go slow."

Before Sara could tell him it was okay—that she didn't want him to go slow—he surged forward in one smooth movement and buried himself deeply inside her. Sara gasped and her head fell back against the sofa. He filled her completely, and the sensation of his hard length inside her was almost unbearable. He moved in a series of bone-melting thrusts and stroked his hands over her ribcage to cup her breasts, gently squeezing her nipples until she arched upward with a strangled cry of pleasure.

"That's it," he coaxed, his voice deep and sexy.

Sara watched his face grow taut as his movements grew stronger. She could actually feel him swell inside her, and her own flesh clutched at him greedily. But when he slid a hand to where they were joined and then angled his hips for maximum penetration, she couldn't suppress the orgasm that had been building. Pleasure crashed over her, wracking her body with delicious spasms.

Above her, Rafe's expression was almost fierce as he watched her. As she climaxed around him, he spread her knees wider and pressed even deeper. Through a haze, Sara watched as he gave a hoarse shout and stiffened, the cords in his strong throat standing out as he thrust one last time. Then he collapsed over her.

Eventually Rafe shifted, drawing her legs around him as he cradled her head into his shoulder. Sara felt his lips trace a tender path across her cheek to her temple, and as she wound her arms around his neck, she could feel him trembling. The knowledge that she had done this to him was both humbling and astonishing, and she tightened her arms around him. They lay together for several long minutes before Rafe finally eased himself upward.

"You okay?"

Cool air caressed her overheated skin, making her feel chilled. She nodded, missing his warmth. Rafe left the room to discreetly dispose of the condom, and Sara was acutely aware that she lay sprawled naked across his sofa in the middle of the day. Rolling to her feet, she realized there wasn't even a blanket or throw to wrap around herself. Now that the urgency of release had passed, she felt mildly embarrassed by her own uninhibited behavior. She didn't mind stepping out of her comfort zone, but this was a bit much. She'd stepped so far out that she might as well be in a foreign country. She felt completely out of her element.

Sara heard the toilet in the downstairs bathroom flush, and quickly scrambled for her clothing. By the time Rafe came back into the living room, she had her panties on and her shirt closed. She wasn't certain, but she thought she detected something like disappointment in Rafe's expression.

"I was getting cold, and your leather couch isn't exactly warm and cozy," she said in explanation. "At least, not without clothing." Bending over, she reached for her jeans, letting her hair fall forward to hide her face.

"Well, then, let me keep you warm," he said with an easy smile. "Are you hungry? Can I get you something to drink?"

"No, thanks. I, um, think I'll go take a shower," she demurred and reached for her shoes.

"Hey, wait a minute." Rafe came to stand in front of her, sweeping her hair back with both hands and dipping his head to search her face. "What's going on? I know that whole thing was ridiculously rushed and unromantic, but I'm pretty sure you wanted me, too." His eyes were so full of concern that Sara felt her heart constrict.

"I did," she said quickly. "I do. It's just that you make me want to do things that two days ago I would never have considered doing, and then afterwards I feel so—so—"

She broke off, unable to verbalize how he made her feel. She wasn't even sure she could admit it to herself. He made her forget herself—when she was with him, she seemed to become a different person. Had she wanted to have sex with Rafe in the middle of his living room? Hell, yes. But that didn't keep her from feeling a little unsettled about her own behavior afterwards.

To her dismay, Rafe pulled her roughly into his arms. "I'm sorry," he muttered against her hair. "I'm an insensitive bastard. My only excuse is that I've spent too long in uncivilized parts of the world. I've never met a woman like you, and I forget sometimes that you're not like—" He stopped abruptly.

Sara pulled away from him with a frown. "Like

who?" she asked, a little afraid to hear his answer. Had he been hurt by a former girlfriend? Someone he still cared about?

"Nothing," he replied, and scrubbed a hand across his face. Standing up, he pulled her to her feet. "It's nothing. Go take your shower."

Gathering up her discarded clothing, she made her way quickly up the stairs, aware that Rafe's eyes followed her. Part of her wanted to invite him to join her, to suggest they spend the rest of the day and the coming night in bed together, but then she remembered his last words. *I forget sometimes that you're not like...*

Like *who*?

The unknown answer tormented her, and that scared her more than anything.

RAFE WATCHED HER GO, silently cursing himself for being such a damned moron. He should go after her. He could see she was upset, and if he had any decency in him at all, he'd follow her and assure her that it wasn't her; it was him.

He couldn't stop picturing the incident in the living room, and more than anything, he wanted a repeat performance. Just thinking about Sara spread out on his sofa caused lust to spiral through him. He couldn't get enough of her. Even as he replayed the erotic scenario, he mentally kicked himself for the way he'd treated her. Christ, he'd been so eager to get inside her that he hadn't even considered her feelings. She was so obviously not the kind of woman who engaged in casual sex, and yet he'd taken her on the arm of his couch. He hadn't even bothered to undress completely! He couldn't recall the last time a woman had made him feel this way—as though he had flames licking beneath his skin that only she could extinguish.

Rafe waited until he heard the water in her shower turn on before he went up the stairs to his own room. Stripping out of his clothing, he decided he could use a shower, too, but a cold one. Even after the intense orgasm he'd just had, he wanted her again. Stepping into his bathroom, he was reaching for the shower handle when he paused, and then let out a curse.

He was completely screwed.

Swiftly wrapping a towel around his hips, he strode across the hallway to Sara's room. He hesitated only briefly before opening the door and stepping inside. Her discarded clothing lay in a heap on the floor by the bed. Steam misted through the partially open door to the bathroom, and Rafe was helpless to prevent himself from crossing the room and stepping into the humid bathroom. He could just make out her form through the shower enclosure, her body wreathed in steam. Sucking in a deep breath, he opened the glass door.

Sara whirled around, startled. Her hair was slicked back, darkened by the water, and her eyelashes were spiky with moisture as she stared at him.

"Sara." His voice sounded hoarse. "May I come in?"

She blinked at him, holding a bath scrunchie against her chest that dripped foamy suds over her breasts and stomach. Just when he thought she would refuse, she lowered the scrunchie and stepped back enough to make room for him. Relief surged through him. He let his towel drop to the floor and stepped into the shower, not missing how her gaze dropped to his arousal.

"Rafe…" Her voice was no more than a whisper.

He slid his hands beneath the fall of her wet hair

and lifted her face, feeling the slick slide of her body against his. "You said I make you do things that you'd never have considered doing two days ago. Well, I can say the same thing about you." At her questioning look, he gave her a rueful smile. "Let's just say that you do things to me that no other woman has ever done. You make me crazy."

He searched her eyes, watching as her pupils dilated and her breath escaped on a soft sigh. He lowered his head and slid his lips against hers, softly fusing their mouths together as warm water sluiced over them. She opened for him and he pressed forward, sliding his hands to her back to explore the dips and curves of her shoulder blades and spine.

"Oh," she breathed, dragging her mouth free to press it against his shoulder. "I can't believe you followed me in here. I thought you regretted what happened downstairs."

"What?" He pulled back to look at her in astonishment. "Are you kidding? Lady, that was every dream I'd ever had come true." Stepping back, he spread her arms wide and drank his fill of her. Her breasts were full and lush above a narrow waist and slender hips. "Look at you—you're incredible."

Sara laughed and drew his hands back around her, sliding sensuously against him. "I'm glad you think so."

Her body was wet and warm and supple and it was all Rafe could do not to lift her against the tiled wall and bring her down onto his aching shaft. Instead, he took the scrunchie from her hands and worked it gently across her breasts, watching the streams of water trickle clean paths through the suds to expose the dusky tips. Mesmerized, he worked the rough fabric until his hands were filled with soap before he let it drop to his feet. Then, taking his soapy fingers, he smoothed them over her body, reveling in the warm, slippery feel of her beneath his palms.

Sara made a sound of pleasure and when he eased a hand between her thighs, her head fell back and she widened her stance to allow him better access.

"Christ. You're so soft," Rafe groaned, gently parting her folds. "I could touch you like this forever."

"And I'd let you," she replied with a husky laugh. "Oh, that feels so good."

He supported her around her waist as she leaned back against the tiled wall, but didn't stop the sensuous rhythm of his hand. "And to think," he mused against her mouth, "that I almost let you shower alone."

Sara gasped as he gently bit the side of her throat. "What made you change your mind?"

"The thought of you up here. Alone. Naked."

She laughed softly. "But you've already had your wicked way with me, Sergeant. What more could you possibly want?"

He pulled back to search her face, watching as water streamed from her hair and over her shoulders. He followed one rivulet as it slid down her collarbone and along the slope of her breast before he bent and caught it with the tip of his tongue.

"Oh, there's more," he assured her, drawing her nipple into his mouth and savoring her small gasp. "Let me show you."

MUCH LATER, THEY LAY TOGETHER in Rafe's wide bed. Sara rested her head on his shoulder and trailed a finger up and down the shallow groove that bisected his torso and separated the grid of muscles across his stomach. Outside, it was dark, but the light from the bathroom was enough to illuminate the bedroom and reveal Rafe's features. In the dim light, he looked slightly satanic. Dangerous.

"What are you thinking about?" she asked softly.

He turned his head on the pillow and a small smile lifted one corner of his mouth. "You."

Sara smiled. "Oh yeah? And what are you thinking about me?"

Rolling toward her, he raised himself up on one elbow and stroked her hair back from her face. "I was just thinking that my leave is up in two weeks, but I have some more time coming to me. I could probably request another two weeks without any problem."

"Is that what you want?" she asked carefully.

He blew out a hard breath. "What I want is to have more than just this week with you."

Sara heard the frustration in his voice and warmth unfurled low in her abdomen. He wanted to spend more time with her! The knowledge thrilled her, and yet something inside her hesitated to read too much into his words. He was a Special Ops soldier, after all. What kind of relationship could they really have, beyond a week or two? He would soon be returning to duty, and she didn't know if she was the kind of woman who could sit at home for six months or more, patiently waiting for her man to return. And what if he didn't return? What if he was killed during one of his covert missions? Just the thought of losing him caused a physical reaction; her chest tightened and she couldn't seem to draw a deep breath.

Rolling away from him, Sara swung her legs over

the side of the bed and sat up, struggling to breathe. Behind her, Rafe shifted closer.

"Hey, did I say something wrong? Are you okay?"

She nodded, but didn't look at him. "Yes. I'm just surprised. I mean, you've only known me for a couple of days."

He stroked his knuckles along the side of her arm. "I know you're probably thinking that we jumped into this a little too quickly," he said quietly. "You may even think that I invited you to stay with me for a week just so I could get you into my bed."

Sara gave him a quick smile over her shoulder. "Obviously, I didn't need much persuasion."

"Are you having regrets?"

She turned to face him. "I just can't help but wonder where this is going. I love that you want to spend more time with me, but we both have demanding jobs. Well, okay, yours is a lot more demanding than mine, but even if you can get some additional time off, I don't think my editor will be so accommodating." She gave him a rueful smile. "I'm sure she probably considers this week with you just one big vacation for me. Either way, by the end of the week, I still need to give her a story about you."

With a soft groan, Rafe rolled onto his back and flung an arm over his eyes. "That's right. I almost forgot that you're a journalist. The story comes first, right?"

His voice sounded bitter and Sara frowned.

"That was the deal, Rafe, remember? I agreed to stay with you for a week and in return, you agreed to give me a story."

With a muttered oath, Rafe surged to his feet and strode across the room to stare moodily out the window into the darkness. "So this is nothing more than a business transaction to you, is that what you're telling me?"

Sara drank in the sight of him as he stood gloriously nude, bathed in a muted amber glow from the streetlamps. Shadows played across his body, casting his muscles into sharp relief and outlining the powerful thrust of his shoulders and the definition of his arms. His body was tightly coiled, and Sara could sense the frustration that simmered in the air around him. She stood up, wrapping the sheet around her.

"I didn't make the rules," she reminded him softly. "You did. Those were your terms, not mine. But no... this isn't *just* about the story, and you know it."

When he turned around, his face was cast in shadow so that she couldn't distinguish his features, never mind discern his expression. "What if I asked you to forget about the story and stay with me anyway?" he asked quietly. "Would you do it?"

Sara's breath caught. "I don't know. I have responsibilities. Even if I wanted to, my editor is counting on this story and I can't just say no to her. I need this job. I have to give her that story, Rafe."

Rafe scrubbed a hand over his short hair and muttered a soft invective. "But why this particular story, Sara? And who is this really important to? You or your editor?"

Sara frowned. "Well, it's important to both of us, but Lauren said the story about the rescue mission would be a major coup for the magazine."

"And what would the story do for you?" His voice was deceptively soft.

Sara cleared her throat. "Well, it would be a coup for me, too. At least from a professional standpoint."

His silence filled the room. "Try to understand, Rafe. Do you know how hard it is to get the inside scoop on a story like yours?"

"I'm trying," he said grimly. "I know I said I'd give you the story if you stayed with me, but I'd rather you were here because you wanted to be with me, and not because I'm going to give you some inside scoop on a classified mission."

Sara recoiled, feeling as if she'd been slapped. "That's not fair," she breathed. "You know I want to be with you. But why can't I also want the story? Why can't I have both?"

She heard him laugh softly. "Because then I'll never be sure, will I?"

"Sure about what?" But she already knew. He would never be sure if she was with him because she wanted to be with him, or because she wanted the story that only he could give her. Sara started to get angry. He was implying she was only slightly better than Colette, selling herself for profit. "What's going on, Rafe? Why does it bother you so much that I want that story? You know my background—I'm a journalist. This is what I do, but you've made it pretty clear that you don't have much use for journalists." She paused, but he didn't speak. "Why?"

"I'll tell you why," he said on a soft snarl, crossing the room and coming so close that a deep breath would have brought her breasts into direct contact with his chest. "One of the aid workers that we rescued in Pakistan turned out to be a reporter."

Sara stared at him, uncomprehending. "So?"

"So my men risked their lives to save her pretty little ass, but being rescued wasn't her priority."

Sara stared at him. "So what was she after?" she asked, but she already knew.

"She was trying to get pictures of the Taliban, but all she did was succeed in getting herself and the other aid workers captured. Even after we extracted her and the others, she tried to document the rescue mission with her camera. Because of her and her idiotic desire *to get the story,* my men were injured and very nearly killed. Worse, if we hadn't confiscated everything she owned and convinced her editor that the article would blow our cover and jeopardize future missions, she would have published her story—complete with photos—on the front page of some national news magazine."

He moved away from her and Sara sagged against the wall, clutching the sheet against her. She understood now why he had been so abrupt with her that first night, when she'd been introduced to him as a writer for *American Man* magazine. She also understood why he'd walked away from her at the Pavilion Café when she'd asked him to tell her about the rescue. Given his experience, he had no reason to trust her. In fact, she hadn't really given him any reason to think she was much different than the other journalist.

"I'm not like her," she finally managed, her voice sounding strained. "I already told you that I would keep your identity a secret, and that I wouldn't publish your picture. I just wanted to hear about the rescue."

"And now you have," Rafe grated. He turned back toward her, his expression predatory. "Which leads me back to a question you never answered—how did you find out about my involvement with the rescue in the first place? That mission was so covert that only a handful of men at the Pentagon knew about it. Who is your 'reliable source'? Some other poor bastard you slept with in order to get your story?"

"Rafe, please don't do this." She knew he didn't really mean the things he was saying, but the words still had the power to hurt her.

He blew out a hard breath. "You're right. You know what? I'm sorry. It's late, and we could both use a good night's sleep." He considered her bleakly. "You're welcome to stay in this room. I'll sleep downstairs on the sofa. Don't worry—this won't happen again."

Sara blinked. He couldn't even stand to be in the same room as her and the knowledge caused her stomach to twist. She watched as he snatched a clean pair of boxers from his dresser and pulled them on. It wasn't until he was reaching for an extra blanket at the foot of the bed that reality kicked in.

"No, don't leave," she said, putting out a hand to forestall him.

He paused and gave her a questioning look. "You want me to stay?"

Pulling the sheet tighter around herself, she indicated the bedroom door. "I only meant that I'll sleep in the spare room. There's no need for you to sleep on the couch."

"Thanks," he muttered, sounding anything but grateful.

Sara hesitated, wishing she could think of something to say, wanting just to go back to the way things had been fifteen minutes earlier. She even briefly considered telling him that she'd ditch her plans to write the story if he would just let her stay with him for the night, for two weeks. Forever.

But she knew she couldn't do that. If she didn't have

a story for Lauren by the end of the week, she could lose her job. And if she got fired then she'd have no choice but to go back home to Pennsylvania. Journalists were a dime a dozen in Washington, and without any references or high-profile stories in her portfolio, she'd have a tough time finding another job.

Blowing out a hard breath, she turned away. "I'll see you in the morning," she murmured, and without waiting for a response, she fled to the spare room, closing the door behind her and climbing naked between the cold sheets.

She lay curled on her side, imagining Rafe across the hallway, and wishing she weren't such a coward. Wishing she had told him that the story didn't matter, that being with him was more important. But she hadn't. Instead, she'd chosen her job over Rafe. With a groan, she turned her face into her pillow. She didn't even really like her job. But she needed the money and the connections. Bunching the pillow beneath her head, she silently acknowledged that in that respect, she wasn't so very different from Colette, after all.

12

SARA SPENT A RESTLESS NIGHT, unable to sleep. After several hours spent replaying the scene with Rafe over and over again in her head, and berating herself for handling it so poorly, she gave up altogether. Instead, she pulled her laptop out to check emails, and then remembered the memory stick hidden in her pocketbook.

But, after inserting the stick into the laptop and opening the file, she wasn't any closer to knowing what information resided on the data card. The file was encrypted, and Sara had no clue how to decipher it. Opening her purse, she replaced the memory stick in the zippered side pocket and returned to her mail.

In the morning, Sara repacked her belongings into her overnight bag, and tried to convince herself that she was making the right decision in returning to her own apartment. This whole thing had been a huge mistake. Their lives were too divergent ever to make a relationship work. Rafe despised journalists, and she wasn't sure she could handle those long periods when he would be gone on a mission. Not to mention, he had no right to make her choose between himself and her career. After all, she wasn't thrilled that his job put him in harm's way, but she wasn't about to ask him to leave the military for her.

Then there was the whole issue with the story. It was clear Rafe wouldn't provide her with any information and she had promised to keep his identity a secret, so what did that leave her with? She'd been fooling herself in thinking this story would make a difference to her career. There was no story, and she needed to go back and tell Lauren so, even if it meant she might lose her job.

Drawing a deep breath, she made her way downstairs, where she could hear Rafe moving around. She was apprehensive about facing him after the previous night. What if she apologized and told him what she intended to do, and it made no difference? She wasn't sure she could handle his rejection. No, it was better if she just left and chalked the entire thing up as a mistake.

Rafe was pouring two mugs of coffee as she entered the kitchen. His black gaze slid to her overnight bag and laptop case as she set them down on the floor. He didn't say anything, but Sara didn't miss how his jaw tightened. He hadn't shaved, and dark stubble shadowed his chin. As he handed her a mug of coffee, she couldn't help but notice the lines of strain etched around his mouth. He looked as terrible as she felt.

"Thanks," she murmured, accepting the mug and curling her hands around its warmth. She couldn't bring herself to meet his eyes, too afraid of what she might see in his expression. The tension in the small kitchen was palpable.

He set his own mug down on the island. "Sara, about last night—"

Her cell phone rang, startling her so that she sloshed hot coffee over her fingers. "Oh!"

Rafe took the mug from her and she swiped her hand across the seat of her jeans as she bent to retrieve the phone from her handbag. She didn't recognize the number on the display.

"Hello?"

"Sara Sinclair?"

"Yes?"

"This is Detective Paul Anderson with the Metropolitan Police Department. Your neighbor, Mrs. Parker, gave me your cell phone number."

Sara felt her heart lurch. "Is she okay?"

"She's fine. She called us because somebody burglarized your apartment overnight. We'll need you to come home to verify if anything is missing and to file a report."

"My apartment was broken into?" she repeated blankly.

"Yes, ma'am. Your neighbor said you're away on vacation. When do you expect to return?"

Sara put a hand to her forehead, only distantly aware of Rafe coming to stand close to her. "I'll leave right now. I mean, I'm staying with a—a friend. I'll be there in forty minutes."

Ending the call, she looked up at Rafe, feeling a little dazed. "Someone broke into my apartment. I have to go."

"I'll drive you."

"No—I mean, I can drive myself. There's no need for you to come with me."

"That wasn't a suggestion, Sara. I'm driving you, and that's the end of it. Leave your things here," he said, as she bent to retrieve her overnight bag. "If someone burglarized your place, there's no way you're staying there."

Sara straightened. "Right. Of course."

Rafe was grimly silent on the ride to her apartment. When they arrived at her building, Sara was surprised to see there were no police cruisers in sight.

"I'm sure the detective said he would be here," she said, getting out of the car. "Maybe they got another call."

"Trust me, there's a detective upstairs," Rafe said, indicating she should precede him up the stairs.

Sara turned to look at him. "How do you know?"

"There's an unmarked car parked on the curb. From the make and model, I'd say it belongs to your detective."

As they reached the fourth floor, Sara realized he was right. Her apartment door stood open, and Sara could hear voices coming from inside. Entering her apartment, she stopped short and her hand flew to her mouth. Her apartment looked as if a cyclone had hit it, with furniture overturned, and books and photos strewn across the floor. Her small desk had been pillaged and the drawers upended. Even her tiny kitchen hadn't been spared, with utensils and broken dishware littering the ground.

"Oh my God," she breathed, lifting a picture from the floor. The frame was broken and the glass cracked, and Sara felt the hot sting of tears as she gently traced her finger over the photo of her father. Standing up, she looked helplessly at Rafe.

"Who would do this? Why would anyone do this?"

Mrs. Parker stood in the center of the mess, wearing a flowered bathrobe, flanked by two men, one of whom was taking notes in a small book. Sara clutched the broken picture to her chest and stared around her, shocked by the condition of her apartment. Rafe put an arm around her shoulders and she was grateful for his protective bulk.

"Miss Sinclair?" One man stepped toward her and flipped open a leather wallet to reveal an official-looking identification card and a badge. He looked vaguely familiar, but Sara couldn't recall where she might have seen him before. "I'm Detective Anderson and this is my partner, Detective Michaels."

"Oh, my poor dear," exclaimed Mrs. Parker, picking her way over the debris to take one of Sara's hands in her own. "I heard some noises just after midnight, but I thought it was the young people who live beneath me. You know how they like to party."

Sara nodded mutely.

"Then when I went out to get my newspaper this morning, I saw your door was partially open, and thought you had returned. But when I pushed the door open, this is what I found." She patted Sara's hand reassuringly. "Thank goodness you weren't home. I hate to think what might have happened."

Sara squeezed the older woman's fingers. "I'm just glad you didn't decide to go investigate in the middle of the night. Thank you for calling the police."

Mrs. Parker smiled. "That's what neighbors are for. Well, you have your hands full, so I'll leave you. Call me if you need anything."

"Thank you," Sara replied, watching the elderly woman as she left.

"Miss Sinclair," interrupted the other detective,

"we'll need you to take an inventory of your belongings to determine if anything is missing."

Sara nodded and placed the picture of her father carefully on the bookshelf. "Okay, but I won't know for sure until I get everything cleaned up and put away. It might take a few days."

"No problem." The detective hesitated. "Can you think of any reason why someone would want to break in?"

"No." Sara indicated her ruined apartment. "I don't own anything of value. Even my jewelry is mostly costume jewelry."

With a gasp, she remembered the Carolina Herrera gown she had worn to the Charity Works Dream Ball. She hadn't yet had an opportunity to return it to her friend, and she only hoped the burglars hadn't taken it. The gown was worth thousands, and she couldn't afford to replace it if it had been stolen.

Shaking off Rafe's arm, she pushed past the detectives to her bedroom, stunned to see that her dresser and closet had been thoroughly ransacked, as well. But she let out a sigh of relief when she found the beautiful cobalt gown on the floor, still in its protective garment bag. Sara lifted it carefully in her arms. The three men had followed her into the room, and she looked at them in confusion.

"This gown is easily worth five thousand dollars. If the robbers were looking for something they could sell for cash, why not take this?"

A ghost of a smile touched Rafe's mouth. "Obviously, your burglar has no appreciation for high fashion."

"They were likely looking for smaller items, like electronics, that they could easily remove from the premises," said Detective Anderson. "Do you own anything of that nature, Miss Sinclair? A laptop, or an iPad, perhaps?"

Sara was about to say that her laptop was at Rafe's house, when Rafe smoothly interrupted.

"I think Sara needs some time alone right now. Why don't I bring her down to your station later, and then she can fill out a report and answer any other questions you might have?"

The two detectives glanced at each other, before Anderson turned to Rafe. "I'm sorry—I didn't get your name."

"That's because I didn't give it."

The other detective gave a soft laugh and scratched the bridge of his nose. "Well, we'd have more to go on if Miss Sinclair could just give us this information now."

"I understand, but I don't see any benefit in putting her through an interrogation right now. I'll bring her down later this morning, I promise. That will give her time to put together a list of missing items."

Rafe's voice was polite, but there was no mistaking the steely edge to it. The two detectives must have realized that they wouldn't get far by persisting, and the first one snapped his small book shut.

"Fine." He turned to Sara, but his expression was one of irritation. Withdrawing a small case from his pocket, he withdrew a business card and handed it to her. "Here's my card. Call me before you come down."

Rafe showed them out, closing the apartment door firmly behind them. Laying the gown across the bed, Sara followed him into the living room, stepping carefully over the mess on the floor.

"Why was he so interested—" she began, but Rafe stopped her with a finger across his lips.

Drawing her close, he leaned down so that his mouth was at her ear. "Don't say anything about the detectives," he whispered. "Complain about the mess, but don't mention anything that might have been stolen, or speculate on what the robbers were looking for. And talk loudly."

Pulling back, he raised his gaze to the ceiling and pointed silently to the small overhead light mounted there.

"What I don't get," she said, obeying his instructions, "is why they had to make such a mess. I mean, who would keep anything of value in their kitchen drawers?"

As she talked, Rafe carefully unscrewed the globe from the light and examined the wiring, before he deftly removed what looked like a tiny black square. After he replaced the light, Sara watched as he moved around her apartment, locating two more of the small devices, one from the kitchen and another from her bedroom. She didn't need a detective to tell her what they were, and the implications of why they were there terrified her. Still, she managed to keep up a meaningless diatribe on the evils of burglary as she watched Rafe open her freezer. But when he pushed the devices deep into a gallon container of Moose Tracks ice cream, she found herself speechless with surprise.

"Look," he said easily, closing the freezer, "I can see you're upset. It doesn't look like they took anything of value. Why don't we leave this mess for now? Let me buy you breakfast, and then we can find a decent hotel for you to stay at, at least until this place is habitable. You should probably pack a bag for a couple of nights."

Sara wasn't fooled, his easy going manner was only for the benefit of any other listening devices that he might have overlooked.

"Right. Good idea." She left him in the kitchen and returned to her bedroom. Her small suitcase had been dragged from beneath her bed, and it took no more than a few minutes to throw several outfits into the case and zipper it closed. She hefted the suitcase in one hand and then, on impulse, draped the blue ball gown over her free arm.

Rafe arched an eyebrow when he saw the gown. "Planning on going to a ball?" he asked.

Sara gave him a tolerant look. "I'm not taking any chances. They didn't take the gown this time, but they might change their minds if they come back."

"They're not coming back," he said grimly. "Let's go." He took the suitcase from her hand and indicated she should precede him out of the apartment, before he closed and locked the door behind them.

"Fine. And by the way, that was a perfectly good container of ice cream that you ruined," she said as they made their way down the staircase.

"That's a matter of opinion," he retorted. "Now if you'd had a gallon of butter pecan ice cream in that freezer, I might agree."

RAFE WAS GLAD TO SEE A SMILE touch Sara's mouth at his quip. Her face had lost all color when they'd entered her apartment, and even now she was too pale for his liking. They reached his car, and he scanned the street for any sign of the detectives. Their car was nowhere in sight, but every instinct told him they were being watched.

As he slid in behind the steering wheel, Sara leaned

forward and buried her face in her hands. "Oh my God," she said, dragging in a shaky breath. "What is happening to my life?"

"Hey." Reaching across the center console, Rafe hauled her into his arms and pressed her face against his shoulder. He breathed in the honey-ginger scent of her hair and rubbed her back. "It's going to be okay, I promise."

Just two hours ago, he'd been certain that Sara was going to walk out of his life. He'd lain awake for the entire night after she'd left, fighting the urge to follow her into the spare bedroom and make love to her. He'd demanded too much of her too soon, and he couldn't blame her for running scared. Maybe it was a direct result of his lifestyle. In his line of work, there wasn't always a guarantee of tomorrow and he'd learned that if you wanted something, you needed to take hold of it with both hands. He'd said things the previous night that he regretted, things he couldn't take back. But he intended to show Sara that what they had was more than just a one-night stand. He wanted her in his life. More importantly, he needed to be in hers. There was no way he was letting her out of his sight.

"Are you okay?" he asked, tipping her face up so that he could search her eyes.

She nodded, but she wouldn't look at him. "I'm okay. I just can't believe that someone broke into my apartment and worse, that someone planted those—those *bugs*. Who would do that?" She looked at him now. "And how in the world did you know they were there?"

Reluctantly, Rafe released her and started the car. "Let's go for a drive."

He maneuvered the car onto the expressway and

drove for several miles until they reached a major shopping district. Only then did he pull off the highway and follow the signs toward a large mall. He sensed Sara's curiosity as he pulled the car into a parking garage, checking his mirror frequently to ensure they hadn't been followed. Driving to an upper level, he pulled into a vacant parking spot and turned off the engine.

Sara raised an eyebrow. "We're going shopping?"

"Not exactly. We're just going to do an exchange of merchandise."

Rafe got out of the car and carefully began inspecting the undercarriage and wheel wells. Sara got out and crouched beside him as he reached beneath the car and felt blindly with his hand.

"What are you looking for?" she asked.

His fingers closed around a small disk and with a grunt of effort, he peeled it from the undercarriage and rocked back on his heels, opening his hand to reveal what looked like a chunky memory stick.

"What is that?" she asked.

"It's a mini GPS tracker." He angled his head to look at her. "Somebody wants to keep tabs on us. Or on you."

Sara's eyes narrowed. "But that means…did the detectives put that there?"

"Yeah, that's my guess."

"Why are they interested in knowing your whereabouts?"

"Sweetheart, they're not interested in me. It's you they want, but they're in for a big disappointment," Rafe said, and leaning over, he clapped the tracker to the undercarriage of the car parked next to them. "Now let's get out of here."

He maneuvered the car out of the parking garage,

using an alternative exit that put them on a different expressway than the one they'd come in on. He kept an eye on his rearview mirror, but he couldn't detect any signs that they were being followed. After several miles, he allowed himself to relax fractionally.

"I thought I recognized one of the detectives, but I couldn't recall from where," Sara mused. "But it just came to me."

"He was one of the men in the alley the day I kissed you," Rafe said grimly.

"That's right. What about the other guy? Detective Michaels?"

"Also in the alley."

"I don't get it."

Rafe shook his head. "I don't either. My first thought was that they're not real detectives, but all their equipment is real. My guess is that they're working for someone, and they're after your laptop. Any thoughts on why?"

He glanced over at Sara to see her digging through her pocketbook. She withdrew her hand and held a small memory stick. "I think they might be after this."

Frowning, Rafe took it from her. "Where did you get this?"

"Juliet gave it to me. She called it an insurance policy. I tried to open it, but it's encrypted. I have an idea what's on this stick, but I can't confirm it."

On a sudden inspiration, Rafe veered off the expressway.

"Where are we going?" Sara asked. "This isn't the way to your place."

"We're not going to my place." He glanced over at her. "Those two clowns—whoever they are—will have run my license plate. By now, they know who I am and where I live and they'll be watching the house."

"So where are we going?"

"I have a buddy who's deployed right now. We'll stay at his place until we figure out what's going on." He glanced over at her. "He's a computer whiz, and he has the equipment we need to read this memory stick."

"Will we be safe?"

Reaching over, Rafe closed his hand around hers and squeezed her fingers. "I'll never let anything happen to you."

13

SARA GAZED OUT THE WINDOW as they drove through the city, thinking about what Rafe had said. Someone had hired the detectives to follow her, to ransack her apartment. She knew what they had been looking for. The memory stick that Rafe had tucked into his pocket. She even knew who had hired them.

Edwin Zachary.

She shivered. The man had enough money to buy his own country and enough political clout to run it. Rafe had promised to keep her safe, but she wasn't sure anyone could protect her from someone like Edwin.

They'd been driving for almost twenty minutes, and the neighborhoods were becoming more affluent. She didn't know where Rafe was taking her, but the thought of spending another night under the same roof with him unnerved her. She'd spent most of the morning replaying the events of the previous night and wishing she could do them over. She'd quit the magazine if it meant she could spend just one more week with him. She'd tell him that if he had to deploy, then she'd wait for him to come home.

"Are we going to stay at your friend's place overnight?" she finally asked.

"Yeah. There's plenty of room." He glanced over at her. "Is that a problem?"

"No, I'm just surprised that you still want to help me. To be with me."

"You think I don't want to be with you?" he asked, looking at her in astonishment.

"Well, after last night..."

He gave a soft, disbelieving laugh. "After last night, I can't think about anything *but* being with you. As often as possible."

Sara stared at him, and warmth flooded her veins. "But I thought—you despise journalists. You all but said so."

"I said a lot of things last night that I shouldn't have." He glanced at her, his expression rueful. "My only excuse is that I wanted to spend more time with you, and I was angry and frustrated by the fact that you were being so damned *rational*."

Sara swallowed hard, pushing down the small bud of hope that threatened to blossom inside her. "I want you to know that I didn't sleep with you just to get the story."

"I'm glad to hear it," he said drily.

They fell into silence again, and soon pulled off the main road and onto a tree-lined side street of nineteenth-century brownstone buildings. Sara peered out the window, taking note of the street name. Rafe parked along the curb and peered up at one of the brick buildings.

"Here we are," he announced.

"Wow. This is a pretty posh address," Sara commented. "Exactly who is your buddy related to that he can afford to live here?"

Rafe chuckled. "Trust me—he's not living beyond his means."

"Is he a soldier in your unit?"

"Yeah. He's a total pain in the ass, but he occasionally comes in handy."

"Like now. Will he mind that we're using his place?"

"Definitely not."

Clutching the ball gown over her arm, Sara followed him up the steps. Putting down her suitcase, he fished through his set of keys and inserted one into the heavy front door.

"Lego has the penthouse apartment," Rafe said with a grin, taking the ball gown from her and tossing it over one broad shoulder before picking up her suitcase again. "But there's no elevator."

"Imagine that," Sara said with a small smile.

But when they reached the penthouse, Sara wasn't sure if she should laugh or cry. "You're kidding. We can't stay here."

Rafe laid the gown over the arm of a nearby sofa, before moving to a security system beside the door and punching in a coded number. "Why not?"

"Rafe, it's a studio apartment." She gestured around the open space. "There's absolutely no privacy. There's not even a separate bedroom. I really think we should just go to a hotel."

As studio apartments went, it had plenty of room, but there was no question it was a bachelor pad. A mountain bike was hung upside-down by its wheels on one wall and pair of skis and a snowboard leaned against a corner. The wall opposite the sofa was dominated by an enormous flat-screen television, and small, expensive speakers had been mounted around the room for maximum sound effect. A large desk stood against the far wall, sporting an array of high-tech computer equipment. Over the desk was an enormous, framed poster of Jessica Simpson. Her impressive breasts were shown to full advantage in an American-flag-patterned bra, and she wore a pair of camouflage army fatigues that were unbuttoned and peeled downward to reveal her star-spangled bikini underwear. Sara gave a soft huff of laughter. Definitely a bachelor pad.

"I can protect you better here," Rafe said absently, throwing the deadbolt on the door and walking over to close the shades on the enormous windows. "Besides, a hotel wouldn't be any different, since I wouldn't let you have your own room. At least here there's a kitchen, and Lego keeps a stash of weapons under the floorboards. The couch opens into a bed," he continued. "There's a decent bathroom. I'll pick up some food and a bottle of wine. What more could you want?"

Sara gave him a disbelieving look. "A stash of weapons under the floor? Really? You're kidding, right?"

He threw her a swift grin. "No. But we won't need them."

Because you have me. He didn't say the words, but they hung there in the air between them. She knew instinctively that he would use his own body to protect her, if necessary. The thought that she might have put him in danger caused her stomach to tighten into a sick knot of anxiety.

Misreading her expression, he came to stand in front of her and put his hands on her shoulders. "It'll only be for a couple of days."

"So I guess that fact that I don't have any pajamas with me won't be a problem," she said, slanting him a smile.

Rafe groaned and his hands slid around to frame her jaw. His eyes traveled hungrily over her face until they came to rest on her mouth. "Definitely not," he said, his voice husky, and dipped his head to cover her mouth in a kiss that was both tender and possessive.

Sara leaned into him, sliding her hands along his ribcage and reveling in his hardness and strength. Too soon, he pulled away.

"I could easily get sidetracked with you," he murmured, stroking his thumb along her cheek, "but there are a few things we need to figure out first. Like what's on that memory stick."

Pulling her scrambled thoughts together, Sara stepped out of his arms. "Right."

Rafe switched the computer on, and Lego's screen saver appeared. Sara moved closer to see the crosshairs of a rifle move across the screen until it came to rest on the silhouette of a man. As soon as the crosshairs centered on the figure, the screen erupted in a series of simulated explosions and a coating of red blood slowly dripped over the screen. Then it cleared and the process started all over again.

"Gross," Sara murmured. She suspected that Lego was younger than Rafe. But he certainly knew computers. His system was expensive and he had several peripherals that Sara couldn't even identify.

Rafe pulled a second chair over to the computer and gestured for Sara to sit down. She watched as he inserted the stick into the port and with several deft keystrokes, opened the file.

"You make it look so easy," she said. "I swear, when I tried to look at the information, it was nothing but a scrambled mess of letters and numbers."

Rafe nodded. "That's why I suggested we use Lego's system."

There was one file on the memory stick, entitled simply Client List. Sara held her breath as Rafe opened it, and then sat back in dismay. The list contained hundreds of names, in alphabetical order. Beneath the names were the dates of each alleged Glass Slipper encounter, along with the name of the girl and how much the client had paid for her services.

Sara's eyes widened as she scanned the list. The names included some of the most powerful and influential men in Washington, both in the White House and the Pentagon, as well as in some of the nation's top financial investment firms. They were politicians and CEOs and high-ranking military officers. Some of the men had paid tens of thousands of dollars to the Glass Slipper Club. Some had been members for years. Sara felt slightly ill.

"Jesus H. Christ," Rafe breathed. "No wonder someone wants this."

"Stupid, stupid, stupid," Sara muttered, pushing to her feet and pacing the small apartment. Why had she ever accepted the memory stick from Juliet? If she'd had any idea of what the stick contained, she wouldn't have touched it with a ten-foot pole. No wonder Juliet had feared for her life. Sara struggled to think coherently.

"Sara, listen to me," Rafe said urgently, grasping her by the shoulders and turning her to face him. "Nothing is going to happen to you, I promise. I'll protect you with my own life if I need to."

"God, Rafe."

He led her over to the sofa and made her sit down. "Who knows you have the memory stick? Did you tell anyone about it?"

Sara shook her head. "No."

"Did anyone know about your meeting with Juliet?"

"I don't think so. I can't remember!"

"Think, Sara. This is important."

Sara fought to collect her thoughts, going back through the events of that day. "I told my editor about seeing Edwin Zachary with Colette, but not about the black book."

"Did you tell her about Juliet?"

"No. Lauren was so sure there was no story there, but I *knew* there was. I wanted to follow it on my own, to show Lauren that I could be a true investigative journalist and give her a story that was even bigger than your rescue of the aid workers." She smiled apologetically. "Sorry."

"No, that's good," he assured her. "The fewer people who know about what you've found, the better."

"Rafe," she said urgently, laying a hand on his arm, "I called Juliet's phone! I identified myself by name and even taunted Juliet about the black book and how I could identify each of the clients. I did everything but threaten to expose the men involved, and it was only later that she told me her phone was probably bugged. Whoever was listening to that phone call definitely sees me as a threat." She groaned and covered her face with her hands. "The worst part is that I only have myself to blame."

"Listen, I have a plan," Rafe said, gently tugging her hands away and giving her a reassuring smile. "Juliet was right about this stick being your insurance policy. Right now, it's the only thing that's keeping you safe. Whoever is after this information won't risk killing you without knowing where the memory stick is."

Sara wanted to throw up. Images of being kidnapped and tortured flashed through her mind. She was in way over her head, and Rafe was her only lifeline. "Okay, I'm listening."

"We'll put the stick somewhere safe, where nobody can get their hands on it. Then you're going to call Detective Anderson and tell him that you think you know why someone broke into your apartment."

"You want me to tell him about the jump stick?"

Rafe smiled. "Yes. But I want you to tell him that you're going to meet with your editor and share it with her before you do anything else. He'll try to persuade you to bring it to him right away, even offer to come and get you. Don't agree to anything."

Sara drew her breath in. "But if Detective Anderson really has been hired to silence me, won't that make him a little anxious to get the job done?"

"That's what I'm counting on," Rafe said grimly. "If we can lure him out, then I'll take it from there. We need to find out who hired him."

"I'm not sure I like this idea," Sara fretted. "I feel like bait."

"He won't be given a chance to hurt you, I promise," Rafe said. "But right now, he's our best shot at finding out who's behind this."

"So I'm going to meet with Lauren in a public place, and you believe Anderson will follow me there?"

"If my hunch is right, then I know he will. He has to believe that you're ready to go public with the information, and he'll need to act quickly to stop you." He tipped her chin up and looked directly into her eyes. "But he won't get the chance."

"I believe you," Sara breathed. "Do you really want me to tell Lauren about the memory stick?"

Rafe was silent for a minute. "That's up to you. If you go public, you'll uncover one of the biggest scandals ever to rock Washington."

A story like this could change her career. She could become the most well-known journalist in the country. The words weren't spoken, but they hung there in the air.

"Okay," she murmured. "I understand. When do you want me to call Detective Anderson?"

"Right now."

She didn't know who moved first, but in the next instant she was in Rafe's arms. Her hands smoothed over the big muscles of his back as she burrowed into his warmth, breathing in his scent and savoring the feel of his hard body against hers.

"I'm sorry," she said against his shoulder. "I'm sorry I got you into this. I'm sorry about last night. I'm sorry that I disappointed you."

He framed her face in his hands and bent down to look directly into her eyes with exasperation. "What are you talking about? First of all, I chose to get involved. I *wanted* to get involved. Second of all, we both said things last night that we didn't mean. I get that. But it doesn't mean we can't start over, right? Third, you did *not* disappoint me."

Sara drew in a shaky breath. "Really?"

"Absolutely." He searched her face for a long moment and when he spoke, his voice sounded rough. "You blew me away."

Sara felt as if he were looking into her very soul, and her breath caught. Her gaze drifted over his face, taking in the chiseled cheekbones and strong jaw, and the mouth that could go from hard to sensual in a heartbeat. His eyes were black velvet.

"Rafe…"

With a soft groan, he bent his head and covered her mouth with his own. His lips were warm and demanding, and Sara leaned into him, sliding her hands around to his back to press him closer.

He pulled away first, but his eyes were hot when he looked down at her. "Save that thought," he said on a husky note. "Call Lauren and set up a time to meet with her. Choose a public place, and then call Detective Anderson."

He waited while Lauren dialed her editor. Lauren picked up on the third ring.

"Lauren," she said gratefully. "Thank goodness."

"Sara? Are you okay?" Lauren asked. "You sound terrible."

"Yes, I'm fine, but I have to talk to you."

"Good. Because I need to talk to you, too. Meet me at the Singapore Bistro. I'll buy you a drink. You sound like you could use one."

"You want to meet right now?" Sara glanced at her watch, surprised to see it wasn't yet four o'clock. She gave Rafe a questioning look and he nodded.

"Sure, why not?" Lauren continued. "I'm having a cocktail and I hate to drink alone."

Sara held her hand over the speaker. "She's been drinking," she mouthed silently to Rafe. He shrugged.

"Maybe we should wait until tomorrow," Sara suggested hopefully. "We could have lunch somewhere."

"Ah, I get it. It's that handsome devil in dress blues, isn't it? What, does he have you tied up while he has his wicked way with you?"

"No, of course not," Sara exclaimed, but felt her face grow hot at the pictures her imagination conjured up. She glanced at Rafe to see if he had overheard the other woman's comment.

"Then put on some lipstick and come join me for a drink. I'm going to make you an offer that you can't refuse."

"Really? That sounds intriguing. Where are you again?"

"The Singapore Bistro on Nineteenth Street. I'll be at the bar."

Sara closed her phone and looked at Rafe. "She wants me to join her for a drink at the Singapore Bistro right now."

Rafe glanced at his watch. "Okay, let's go. You can call Detective Anderson on the way over. I'll wait outside the restaurant for you. If Anderson shows up, he'll never make it inside."

Once inside Rafe's car, Sara withdrew the business card that Detective Anderson had provided to her earlier that day, and dialed his number, ensuring the volume was high so that Rafe could hear everything.

"Detective Anderson."

"Yes, this is Sara Sinclair. We met this morning when my apartment was broken into?"

There was a brief silence. "Yes, Ms. Sinclair! You

never came down to the station as you promised. Is everything okay?"

"Yes. I'm calling because I think I know what the burglar may have been looking for. A—a friend gave me a memory stick with some information on it that could be potentially embarrassing to some people here in Washington. Important people."

"Okay, good. That's excellent news, and it's even more important that you let me help you. Do you, uh, have the memory stick with you?"

She looked over at Rafe and he nodded. "Yes," she replied. "I have it here."

"And where is that, exactly?" He cleared his throat. "I assume you're not staying at your apartment right now?"

"No, I'm staying with a friend."

"Rafe Delgado?"

Sara's gaze snapped to Rafe's and he shook his head.

"No, I'm actually staying with a girlfriend," she fibbed.

"Fine. Give me the address and I'll come pick you up."

"Well, I'm not there right now. I'm on my way to meet my editor. I thought she should see the information and decide if there's a story here or not."

There was silence. "I wouldn't do that, if I were you."

Sara felt her heart stutter. Was that an underlying menace she detected in his voice, or just her overwrought imagination? "Why not?"

"You should turn the data over to the authorities, Sara, and let us handle it. If someone is willing to break into your home to get the information on that stick, then there's no telling what else they might do. There are desperate, deranged people out there, Sara. Let me send a car to pick you up."

Rafe nodded.

"Okay, then." She swallowed hard and gave him the name of the restaurant.

"I'll be there shortly."

Sara hung up and looked helplessly at Rafe. "Are you sure you know what you're doing?"

He pulled the car over to the curb and Sara realized they had arrived. The Singapore Bistro was directly across the street. "This is going to work," he assured her. He glanced at his watch. "Anderson should be here in about fifteen minutes. Go find out what your editor wants, but stay inside until I come get you, okay?"

"Rafe, don't do anything crazy, please?"

"You need to trust me."

"I do." Leaning across the seat, she pressed a soft kiss against his mouth. "I'm trusting you with my life."

LAUREN HAD DEFINITELY had more than her share of lychee martinis by the time Sara found her at the bar.

"Finally, you're here," she said, signaling to the bartender for another drink. "Where's your handsome devil? I thought you were supposed to be shadowing him for the entire week?"

Sara eased herself onto the barstool next to Lauren and accepted the fruity martini that the other woman pushed toward her. "He had some business to take care of tonight, but he's picking me up later."

"Fast worker," Lauren said approvingly. "I told you that he noticed those boobs of yours. Now he's eating out of your hand."

"You said you had an offer for me that I wouldn't be

able to refuse," Sara reminded her, sipping at her drink and ignoring the remark.

"I did. You enjoyed yourself at the Charity Works Dream Ball, didn't you?"

Sara looked at her suspiciously. "Is this a trick question?"

Lauren waved her hand dismissively. "Absolutely not. But there's an upcoming social event that the magazine wants me to cover, and I immediately thought of you."

"Oh?"

"You're a natural. You look fabulous in designer gowns and you have a way with men." She waggled her eyebrows at Sara and took a noisy slurp of her martini. "You're the perfect choice to cover this gala event."

Sara avoided Lauren's eyes and toyed with her swizzle stick. "What is it, exactly?"

"Diane Zachary is hosting a book launch for her good friend, the ambassador to France. Everyone who's anyone is going to be there." Her eyes gleamed. "Including Mr. Edwin Zachary."

"Oh, no!" Sara protested, putting her hands up. "Absolutely not. You'll have to find someone else, Lauren."

Lauren pouted. "Now don't be like that. I don't have anyone else, and I was thinking that after you so gallantly came to his rescue the other night, he might even be willing to give you a few words for the magazine."

Sara groaned, wishing she could get up and walk out. There was no way she could go to a party hosted by Edwin and Diane Zachary. "No, no, no! A thousand times no. I couldn't face him again! He knows that I know he was with a call girl."

"Which is why he'll consent to giving you a few words. He doesn't want you spilling the beans to Mrs.

Zachary, paragon of virtue that she is. The news would destroy her."

"The news would destroy him," muttered Sara. "And his career." Which was why Sara suspected he had hired a couple of thugs to come after her. There was no way she could go to his house. She gave Lauren a pleading look. "I could never face him again. Are you certain there's nobody else who could go? What about you? You could go—he wouldn't refuse to talk with a senior editor at *American Man* magazine."

Lauren gave a bark of astonished laughter and waved her hand in denial. "Oh, no. I most definitely cannot go to that party." She gave Sara a wink and lifted her glass in a toast. "This is your gig, baby. Make the most of it."

"When is it?" Sara asked with a sinking feeling. With luck, she'd have a commitment that she couldn't break.

"Saturday night."

"Lauren, that's just days away! There's no way—"

"This isn't negotiable, sweetie. I need you to go to this party. In fact, I'd consider it a requirement for continued employment. Now drink up."

Sara watched as Lauren raised her martini and tipped it back, swallowing the entire contents in one long swig.

"Can I bring a guest?" she asked abruptly when Lauren set her glass back down and delicately swiped her lips.

"Ah, the marine." Lauren waved her hand in an expansive gesture. "Sure, why not? I'm feeling generous. He cleans up pretty nice, and he'll provide some added clout when you ask Edwin for a few words."

Oh, he would certainly ask Edwin for a few words, Sara thought, warming to the idea. If he didn't kill the man first.

14

STANDING IN A SHADOWED DOORWAY across the street from the Singapore Bistro, Rafe glanced again at his watch. Thirty minutes had passed, yet there was no sign of Detective Anderson, although the restaurant had a steady stream of customers going in and out. He'd parked his car in a small lot farther down the street, where it wouldn't easily be seen if someone were looking for it. Now, as he watched the doorway of the bistro, he worried that maybe he'd been wrong. Maybe Anderson had gone in through the rear entrance, or maybe he'd sent someone else in his place.

Lurid images of Sara in danger haunted him, and it was all he could do to stay where he was and not go charging through the front door of the restaurant. Pulling out his cell phone, he sent her a quick text message.

R U OK?

In less than a minute, a reply came back.

Coming out.

He frowned. What the hell? He'd specifically told her to wait inside the restaurant until he came in to get her. Maybe something had happened. But there was no way he wanted her leaving the restaurant without him right there by her side. He was just leaving the protective shadows when he saw her step out onto the sidewalk. Her coppery hair was bright beneath the exterior lights, and she looked expectantly up and down the street.

Swearing softly, Rafe stepped onto the sidewalk and waited impatiently for a passing car so that he could cross to her.

"Sara," he called. "Wait there, I'm coming over."

She peered across the street at him and waved, and before Rafe could reach her, she stepped forward and off the curb. As if time itself had slowed, Rafe heard the revving of a powerful engine and the squeal of tires. He looked to his left to see a large, dark sedan accelerate from a side street, picking up speed as it approached. With its high beams on, it raced closer, and Rafe realized it was headed directly toward Sara. She had reached the middle of the street and now she stopped, frozen, a deer trapped in the headlights.

Rafe reacted on pure instinct, launching his body in a flying leap across the short distance, his arms locking around Sara as he tackled her. His momentum propelled her backwards and he twisted so that he took the brunt of her weight, landing heavily against the granite curb. Pain exploded along his left side and he felt a whoosh of air across his face as the enormous car narrowly missed them. He lay stunned for a moment, then slowly became aware of Sara lying heavily on top of him.

"Sara." She didn't move and panic seized him. He

struggled to sit up, ignoring the red-hot bolts of pain that stabbed through his chest. "Sara, look at me!"

She lifted her head and raised dazed eyes to his, and he collapsed back against the pavement, weak with relief. He lay there for a moment, dragging air into his aching lungs, his arms clamped tightly around her. She struggled to rise, but he found himself unable to let her go. But then there were people rushing toward them, hands outstretched to help, and he reluctantly released her.

"Jesus, that guy nearly killed you!" exclaimed a young man, lifting Sara to her feet, where she swayed unsteadily. "Are you okay?"

Sara's face was pale as she pushed her hair back and stared in bemusement at the small crowd that had begun to gather. "Yes, I think so."

"Did anyone get a license plate on that car?" Rafe asked, pushing himself weakly to a sitting position. His ribs hurt, and he knew that by tomorrow he'd be sore in a dozen different spots.

"No, it all happened so quickly," the young man said, and leaned forward to brush his hand down the back of Sara's shirt. "You're covered in dirt. And you're bleeding."

Rafe struggled to his feet and heard several people gasp. He pushed the man's hand away from Sara so that he could see for himself where she was injured. Her blue sweater was covered in grit, and she was bleeding from an abrasion on her elbow that extended down her forearm. He examined it despite her protests, satisfied to see it was only a superficial grazing of her skin.

Ignoring his own pain, he cupped Sara's face in his hands. "Look at me," he commanded. She did, her blue eyes filled with concern as her gaze drifted over his features.

"That was the craziest thing I've ever seen," she said, staring at him. "You could have been killed." Her pupils were huge, but at least they were the same size.

"I want you to follow my finger without moving your head," he instructed, watching carefully as she did so.

"I'm okay," she finally said, pushing his hand away. She glanced uneasily at the people around them. "Can we just get out of here?"

"Yeah, sure." He put an arm around her shoulders and carefully checked up and down the street.

"Maybe you should go to a hospital," the young man suggested.

"No, I'm really okay," Sara assured him with a smile.

"Not for you. For him." The young man pointed to Rafe. "You're bleeding, too."

Lifting his arm, Rafe looked down to see his shirt had been torn from his shoulder to his waist. Beneath the shredded fabric, his flesh looked as if it had gone through a cheese grater. Blood oozed from the wounds and he could see bits of gravel embedded in his skin. He didn't think his ribs were broken, but they were definitely bruised.

"Oh, Rafe," Sara breathed, her eyes growing dark with concern. "He's right. We should get you to a hospital."

"I'm fine," he grated. He just wanted to get Sara somewhere safe; for all he knew the bastard in the car could be coming around the block for a second attempt to mow her down. "C'mon," he said, taking her arm, "let's get out of here."

"Are you sure?" she asked as he guided her to where

he'd parked his car and put her into the passenger seat. "You look terrible."

"Yeah, well that little incident just took ten years off my life."

It was no less than the truth. He couldn't remember ever feeling such numbing fear as he had when that car had made a beeline for Sara. He hadn't been sure he could get to her in time, and the images he'd had of her being hit would haunt him for a long time. He grimaced as he eased himself into the driver's seat, pressing a hand against his ribs.

"Rafe, you really should see a doctor." Sara leaned across the seat toward him, her face reflecting her own fear.

"I'm fine."

He started the engine, aware that they were probably being watched and that whoever had tried to run Sara down might very well try to follow them back to Lego's apartment.

"Do you think that car intentionally tried to hit us?" Sara asked as he accelerated onto the expressway.

"Not us," Rafe corrected grimly. *"You."*

"Then you were right about Detective Anderson."

Rafe doubted that Anderson had been driving the Lincoln Town Car that had nearly run her down. But whoever *had* been driving had been waiting for Sara to come out of the restaurant. He'd promised Sara she would be safe, but because of him, she'd almost been killed.

"Whoever was driving that car was there because Anderson told them where you were," he admitted quietly. "I should have seen this coming. I should have been more careful."

"This wasn't your fault," Sara said in an astonished voice. "How could you even think that? You saved my life back there. When I think that you could have been killed…" She gave a visible shiver. "If anyone is to blame, it's me. You told me to stay in the restaurant until you came to get me, but I didn't."

"So what did Lauren want?" he asked, changing the subject.

"She wants me to cover a social event on Saturday night at the home of Edwin and Diane Zachary."

Rafe jerked his gaze to hers, certain she must be kidding. But her expression was so miserable that he knew she wasn't.

"I tried to refuse," she continued, "but Lauren insisted I had to go. Apparently the U.S. Ambassador to France has just come out with a book and the Zacharys are hosting a party to celebrate its release. Lauren suggested that Mr. Zachary might be willing to give me an exclusive interview for the magazine since I know about his, um, extracurricular activities. But I did ask if I could bring a date."

Rafe nodded. "Good girl. But if Zachary is the one who's trying to silence you, I'm not sure I want you in his house. If he feels threatened, there's no telling what he might do."

"I think there will be enough people there that I can avoid any direct contact with him." She gave him a smile. "I'll leave that to you."

"Did you tell Lauren about the memory stick?"

"No. After she asked me to attend the Zachary party, everything else just became a blur." She peered out the window. "Hey, this is the exit to the airport. Where are we going?"

Rafe glanced in the rearview mirror, but there was too much traffic to determine if they were being followed. "I'm not taking any chances with your life again," he muttered. "We'll ditch my car here and take a taxi back to Lego's apartment."

He maneuvered the car to the public parking garage, but instead of entering the garage, he pulled up to the valet-parking kiosk.

"I don't have a reservation and I'm running late," he told the valet. "I'll be returning in three days."

"Very good, sir," the valet said, taking Rafe's credit card.

"Hand me my jacket," Rafe asked Sara. "It's in the back seat."

As the valet ran his credit card, Rafe eased his arm into the leather jacket, wincing at the pain in his rib cage. "We'll go into the airport and then come out downstairs, where the taxis pick up," he told Sara. "I want you to go first and I'll hang back to ensure you're not followed. I'll meet you back at Lego's apartment."

He fully expected Sara to protest and insist that they travel together, but she didn't. Instead, she nodded in agreement. "Okay. Whatever you think best."

As they made their way into the airport, Rafe thought he caught a glimpse of a large, black car pulling slowly into the valet lot and he urged Sara to walk faster.

"This way," he said, leading her along a concourse and then down an escalator. He kept an eye on the level above them for anyone who might be following them, but saw only businessmen and routine travelers.

Once they were on the lower level, they exited the airport and Rafe pulled Sara along the sidewalk to the beginning of the taxi queue. An elegantly dressed couple stood at the front of the line, conversing softly in Lebanese. Holding Sara's hand, he spoke quietly to the couple in their own language and then thanked them when they indicated he should take the next taxi.

Ignoring Sara's astonished expression, he handed her into the taxi and pushed some money and the key to Lego's apartment into her hand. "Do you remember the security code?" he asked in a low voice.

"Yes, but Rafe..." Her gaze moved past him to the couple, who stood watching them with interest. "What did you say to those people?"

"I just explained to them that you need this taxi. No, don't argue. I want you in this taxi, Sara." Leaning in, he gave the taxi driver the address for Lego's apartment and an extra tip. "Keep the change. And don't leave until you make sure she's inside the building, got it?"

The taxi driver nodded, and Rafe stepped back and closed the door, thumping the roof of the cab and watching Sara's pale face through the window as they pulled away. He thanked the Lebanese couple once more, and then walked toward the building blending in with the shadows. He scanned the airport road for any sign of being followed. Only when he was sure that Sara's taxi hadn't been followed did he grab a separate cab for himself.

SARA PACED LEGO'S APARTMENT with her arms around her middle, waiting for Rafe. The incident at the bistro had left her feeling edgy and close to tears. When she finally heard a soft knock at the door, she hurried to turn off the security alarm and throw back the deadbolt.

Rafe entered, quickly closing the door and resetting the alarm.

"Are you okay?" he asked, turning back to her.

"Yes, are you?" She hovered, wanting to touch him. "Here, let me help you with your coat."

She helped ease the leather jacket off, suppressing a gasp as she saw his back and side. Beneath the tatters of his shirt, the oozing blood had dried, caking his skin.

"We need to clean your side," she said, adopting a matter-of-fact tone. "Can you take off your shirt, or should we cut it off?" She put her hands out to help him, but he brushed them aside.

"I can do it myself," he said. "Let me look at your arm."

"Rafe, it's just a scratch. You're the one who needs to be looked at, not me."

But she could see from his expression that he wouldn't be denied, and she reluctantly extended her arm for his inspection. He took it gently in his big hands and examined the scrape. "We should clean this before it gets infected. Lego keeps a first aid kit under the sink. Let me go get it."

Sara pulled her arm back, aware that her skin tingled where his fingers had touched her. "No. Not until we take care of you."

"Sara..." His eyes narrowed sternly.

But Sara refused to be intimidated. "I'm not kidding, Rafe. Take off your shirt."

Rafe laughed softly. "Okay, I surrender. But I have a better idea. Let me take a shower and clean up, and then you can do whatever you like."

"Mmm, that sounds like an invitation," she said teasingly, but she didn't miss how pale he looked beneath his tanned skin, and there were lines of pain etched around his mouth.

She watched as he disappeared into the bathroom, and then opened Lego's dresser and fished through his clothing for something to wear to bed. She found a pair of boxer shorts and a T-shirt for herself, and a pair of soft flannel pajama bottoms and a shirt for Rafe. She could hear the shower running as she located the first aid kit and quickly cleaned the scrape on her elbow and covered it with a bandage. She turned as the bathroom door opened, and her mouth went dry as Rafe emerged wearing nothing but a towel around his lean hips. His short hair glistened with moisture and she saw he had shaved the stubble from his jaw. Her gaze drifted over his broad shoulders and the muscular planes of his chest. Then she noticed how he held his hand to his ribcage.

"Here," she said, pulling a chair away from the small kitchen table. "Sit down and I'll get you some aspirin."

He did as she asked and Sara watched him furtively as she opened a cupboard and pulled down a glass. She didn't miss how he winced as he leaned back in the chair. There was a bottle of whiskey in the cupboard, and on impulse, she lifted it down and poured a shot into the glass, handing it to Rafe along with two painkillers.

He slanted her an amused look. "Thanks."

She watched as he chased the painkillers with whiskey and then took the glass and silently poured him another. He took a swallow, tipping his head back and letting out a grateful sigh. The towel slid open over the hard muscle of his thigh, and Sara had an instant image of herself, naked and straddling his lap. Turning away, she reminded herself that he was injured. What kind of person was she to think about sex at a time like this? But when she glanced back, it was to find him watching her through half-closed eyes. The hunger she glimpsed there caused flickers of heat to lick low through her abdomen and she drew in a steadying breath.

She filled a bowl with warm water and carried it over to the table, laying it beside a clean towel. He watched her closely.

"Lean forward a bit so I can see," she murmured, placing a hand on his shoulder.

He did as she asked and Sara only barely contained a gasp as she saw his back. He'd managed to clean most of the grit from the wound, but there was still gravel embedded where he hadn't been able to reach. The entire area was raw and beginning to bloom purple at the edges.

"Does it hurt very much?" she asked softly, dipping the cloth into the water.

He shrugged. "Only when I laugh."

Carefully, Sara cleaned the abrasion and applied an antiseptic ointment with her fingertips. His skin was hot beneath her touch.

"What about your ribs?" she asked. "Do you think they're broken?" She traced a gentle finger across the bruised flesh.

Rafe shifted uncomfortably. "Cracked, more likely."

Sara came to stand in front of him. "Should we bind them? Would that help with the pain?"

To her surprise, Rafe shook his head and reached for her, grasping her lightly by the waist and pulling her forward. "No, it would actually only make it feel worse. I'll be fine."

He tipped his head back and looked at her, and something in his expression made her breath catch. With nothing but the towel wound around his hips, he looked as if he'd been made for a woman's pleasure, and ribbons of desire slowly unfurled low in her abdomen.

"What else can I do for you?" she asked softly, tracing the back of her fingers along the side of his jaw. "There must be something."

Without breaking eye contact, Rafe slid his fingers into the waistband of her boxers. "There is something," he acknowledged on a husky note, and slowly tugged the shorts down over her hips until they pooled around her ankles. Then he slid his hands around to cup her bottom and urge her even closer.

Sara stepped out of the shorts, a thrill of awareness shooting through her as she carefully straddled Rafe's legs. The movement exposed her to his gaze, and his face reflected masculine appreciation as he smoothed his palms along her thighs.

"Jesus, you're gorgeous," he muttered, and slid his hands up her body to cup her breasts.

Sara sighed in pleasure and covered his hands with her own, encouraging him as he brushed his thumbs across her nipples until they thrust against the fabric of the T-shirt.

"When I think what could have happened to you tonight," he murmured, reaching up to frame her jaw in his hands, leaving the rest of the thought unfinished. "I should never have sent you in there alone."

"You were there when I needed you. You saved my life," she breathed, turning her face into his palm.

"Sara," he groaned, "you're killing me."

Sara laughed softly, knowing he wasn't referring to his injuries. Careful not to put any pressure on his side, she leaned forward and brushed her mouth across his. She felt him smile against her lips and deepened the kiss, sliding her tongue past his teeth to stroke and lick inside his mouth, the way she knew he liked. The wet fusion caused heat to slide through her veins and she squirmed on his lap, acutely aware that only a terrycloth towel separated them.

As if reading her mind, Rafe reached between their bodies and cupped her intimately. Sara shifted to give him better access and he ran a single finger along her cleft, dragging a soft cry of surprised pleasure from her.

"Good?" he rasped against her mouth.

"Yes...yes."

She could feel him against her thigh, heavy and hot, and looked down to see the towel had separated completely and there were no longer any barriers between them. His erection strained upward, dark and glossy, the blunt head like a smooth, ripe plum.

Sara curled her hand around him and felt him pulse strongly against her palm. Liquid heat rushed to her core, flooding Rafe's fingers where he still stroked her. She was on fire, throbbing with excitement.

"Ah, babe," he rasped, leaning forward to rake his mouth over her neck and gently bite her shoulder, "you are so freaking hot. Are you safe if we don't use a condom? I saw birth control pills in your purse."

"Yes," she assured him, the thought of having him inside her causing another rush of moisture. "I'm on the pill."

"You're safe with me," he growled, nibbling on the sensitive skin beneath her ear.

Sara gasped and arched her neck to give him better access, even as she pushed forward to slide herself against his rigid length. Rafe groaned and removed his hand from between her thighs to grasp her by the hips.

"Hold on to me," he said roughly.

Sara braced one hand on his shoulder and half stood, her breath hitching as she positioned Rafe's penis at her entrance and then slowly lowered herself onto him, inch by excruciating inch. She let him fill her, stretching her until she was fully seated against his thighs with his hands cupping her buttocks. Her eyes fluttered closed as she realized the position brought her clitoris into perfect alignment with his pelvic bone. Just the exquisite sensation of rubbing against him caused the inner walls of her sex to tighten in anticipation.

"Oh God," she whispered shakily, meeting Rafe's eyes. "I'm not sure I can last like this."

His face was darkly taut, his muscles rigid as he fought to control himself. "I'm not going to move," he said hoarsely. "Take your time."

Slowly, pressing her bare feet against the floor, Sara raised herself up and slid her arms around Rafe's shoulders, threading her fingers through his damp hair. Her breasts flattened against his chest as she levered herself up and down on his rigid shaft. Rafe slid his hands into her hair and kissed her, softly and languidly, his tongue sweeping against hers in long, sensuous strokes that sent bolts of lust to where they were joined. As Sara pushed downward, she realized that at the end of each thrust she could rub herself against him before pulling back again. With Rafe's tongue in her mouth and his hands squeezing her bottom, she was caught in a vortex of intense pleasure.

"Is this good?" she breathed against Rafe's lips. "Is this what you want?"

"Oh, yeah. Better than good," Rafe groaned, and

used his hands to help lift her up and down, increasing their rhythm as her breathing quickened.

Pressure built where he entered her, and the friction of his flesh moving against hers was more than she could bear. She raised herself up until he was almost free of her body, and then thrust downward, grinding her pelvis against his until pleasure exploded through her. With a soft cry, she clutched Rafe around his neck, shuddering as spasms wracked her body. He gripped her buttocks, pulling her tightly against him as he reached his own climax, thrusting deeply inside her.

Sara collapsed against his chest, her breathing labored. She pressed her hot face into his neck as he stroked her back and murmured soft words against her ear.

For her, this had become more than just sex, more than just a story. She had fallen for Rafe Delgado, hard. And she was more than a little afraid of what would happen to them when this was all over and they returned to their normal lives.

15

"ARE YOU READY FOR THIS?" Rafe asked Sara quietly.

With his car still at the airport and Sara's car still in his garage, he'd hired a private limousine to drive them to the Zachary residence for the book-signing party. Since he was attending the event as Sara's escort and wasn't in an official military capacity, he'd borrowed Lego's tuxedo in lieu of his dress blues. His road rash was still sore and his ribs ached, but not nearly as much as they had the night of the near-accident. Sara was luminous in the blue Carolina Herrera dress that perfectly matched the color of her eyes and displayed her white shoulders and stunning cleavage to full advantage.

She looked at him now as the limo pulled up in front of an impressive brick mansion in the exclusive Kalamora Triangle district. She drew in a steadying breath. "Yes, I'm ready."

"Listen, this place is huge and it shouldn't be too difficult to avoid any direct meeting with Edwin Zachary. The last thing we want is for him to realize you're here."

"But what if he's looked at the guest list? What if

he knows I'm here? I don't even want to be in the same house with him."

Rafe shrugged. "Even if he recognizes you, he won't try anything in his own home."

"You're sure?"

"It would be political suicide. Besides," he said, enclosing her hand in his own, "I'll be right beside you the entire time."

"Do you really think he's behind everything?" she asked.

Rafe thought back to how he'd spent the night of the attempted murder of Sara. After they'd had amazing sex on the kitchen chair, they'd opened the pullout sofa where Sara had fallen into an exhausted sleep.

Rafe had watched her for a long time, unwilling to close his eyes. She'd almost been killed, and as much as he tried, he couldn't dispel the images of her being run down by the car. He'd come so close to losing her. He'd tried to curl up behind her, to pull her against his body and go to sleep, but he hadn't been able to get comfortable. His back and ribs ached enough that he'd finally given up.

After ensuring that Sara was sound asleep, he'd logged onto Lego's computer and inserted the memory stick again. He'd spent hours poring over the names on the client list, trying to determine if anyone besides Edwin Zachary might be behind the attempt on Sara's life. In the end, he'd made a copy of the file before sending the drive to a Special Ops buddy with explicit instructions on what to do if anything happened to him or Sara.

Now, recalling the names on the list, he acknowledged that Edwin Zachary wasn't the only one who stood to lose everything if the information became public.

"I don't know," he finally acknowledged. "But we'll figure it out together, okay?"

She looked out the window of the limousine at dozens of other guests climbing the steps to the mansion. They included some of the wealthiest and most influential people in Washington. She swallowed visibly and then nodded.

"Yes, I'm ready."

They entered the residence and were greeted by Diane Zachary herself. In her early sixties, she was still a beautiful woman and Rafe found himself wondering why Edwin felt the need to solicit call girls when he had such a stunning wife at home. He'd done his research on the Zacharys and he knew that Diane came from old money. A known philanthropist, she sat on over twenty boards and had given away countless millions to the Kennedy Center, to the Lincoln Center, and to Harvard University, to name just a few.

Now she extended her hand to Rafe with a brilliant smile, but Rafe didn't miss how her gaze swept over him.

"Thank you so much for coming tonight, Mr...?"

"Sergeant Rafael Delgado, and this is Sara Sinclair."

Her smile never faltered as she took Sara's hand. "Lovely to meet you, my dear. Thank you so much for coming, and do please enjoy yourselves."

Then they moved past her as she welcomed the next guest, and Rafe felt Sara relax beside him. "See?" he murmured in her ear. "No problem."

They moved deeper into the elegant house and, although Rafe had traveled the world and had even operated out of one of Saddam Hussein's palaces during the Iraq war, he'd never seen such discreet opulence as at the Zachary residence.

"I feel like an interloper," Sara murmured as they accepted a glass of champagne from a passing waiter.

"Why?" Rafe asked, taking her elbow and steering her through the crowded rooms. "You're the most beautiful woman here tonight."

She pulled him to a stop near an ornate fireplace, her expression softening. "Really?"

Rafe raised her hand to his mouth. "Really."

Not for the first time, he wished they were back at Lego's place or, even better, his own townhouse. He wanted just twenty-four hours of uninterrupted time with her. Christ, he wanted a lot more than that. He definitely wanted to know her without the fear that haunted her eyes and without the anxiety that caused her to toss restlessly in her sleep. But first he'd need to find out who was trying to harm her, and eliminate them as a threat.

"This is what we're going to do," he said quietly, snagging an appetizer from a passing tray. "I want to search Edwin's private office. If he's involved, we might find evidence there."

Sara looked carefully around and then pinioned him with a fierce look. "Are you insane? What if we get caught?"

"We won't, because you're going to act as a lookout for me."

She blanched. "Rafe, I can't! I'm not some kind of Special Ops soldier like you are."

"You'll be fine. If anyone asks what you're doing, just say you're looking for the powder room."

The book-signing itself was being held in an enormous formal drawing room, and the line of people waiting to get a signed copy extended out of the door and along a wide hallway. Music played softly in the background, and white-tuxedoed wait staff moved seamlessly through the crowd, offering beverages and food items.

As they made their way past the line of people, Rafe could sense Sara's discomfort and he sympathized with her. He'd attended his own share of balls and soirees, but he'd never been in such an intimate gathering of influential personalities.

"Did you see that?" Sara whispered fiercely, glancing back over her shoulder. "That was the former first lady!"

"Yes, it was," he agreed smoothly, poking his head through a doorway. "Let's try through here."

Glancing back the way they had come to ensure they weren't noticed, Rafe pulled her into what looked like an empty sitting room, with dainty upholstered chairs against one wall and a matching chaise along the other. There was a paneled door on the far side of the room, and Rafe put his ear to the wood before carefully trying the handle. It opened easily beneath his hand.

"This is it," he said softly, indicating Sara should precede him into the room.

An enormous desk dominated the room, with leather club chairs flanking a small fireplace and ornate side tables bearing decanters of liquor and cut glasses.

"Oh, this is lovely," Sara murmured, moving around the room to examine the oil paintings on the walls.

"Sara," Rafe said patiently, nodding toward the door. "Keep an eye out, will you?"

He tested the desk drawers only to find them locked. Reaching into his pocket, he withdrew a small tool and inserted it into the top drawer, maneuvering it carefully until the latch sprang free. Sliding the drawer open, he sifted through the documents inside.

"Hurry," Sara urged, pressing her ear to the door.

Rafe opened the remaining drawers and swiftly sorted through the items, frustrated when he found nothing. Reaching into the very back of the bottom drawer, he withdrew a small metal box and quickly popped the lock.

"Sara, come over here," he called softly.

She did, bending over his shoulder to peer at the photos he held in his hand, displaying her cleavage to his greedy gaze in the process.

"Oh my God," she breathed softly, snatching the photo from Rafe's fingers. "Is that who I think it is?"

"Yep." Rafe met her astonished eyes. "Lauren Black is having an affair with Edwin Zachary, and it looks to me like someone might be trying to blackmail him over it."

The black-and-white photos were grainy, as if they'd been taken from a distance, but there was no mistaking the identities of the two figures locked together in an intimate embrace. Rafe thumbed through the photos, each one more salacious than the previous.

"I can't believe it," Sara said, sounding more confused than surprised. "She's never struck me as the type to have an affair, and certainly not with a married man. No wonder she didn't want to come to the book-signing."

"Yeah, no wonder," muttered Rafe, his mind working furiously. Did Lauren have anything to do with the attempts on Sara's life? It made sense, in a twisted way, since she'd invited Sara to the Singapore Bistro the night the car had nearly run them down. But what would her motive have been? There was something there, Rafe could feel it, but he just couldn't put his finger on it.

"Rafe! Someone is coming," Sara hissed, and then Rafe heard it too—footsteps crossing the outer sitting room toward Edwin's office.

Shoving the box back where he'd found it, Rafe swiftly closed the drawer and caught Sara's hand, dragging her across the room to a closet. Opening the door, he thrust her inside and followed her, pulling the door shut just as the outer door to the office opened. The closet was tiny, and there were boxes near their feet, making it impossible to move without creating noise. Holding Sara against his chest, Rafe laid his fingers over her lips, silently warning her to be quiet.

Easing the closet door open just a fraction, Rafe could see Edwin Zachary clearly. He watched as the other man poured himself a glass from the crystal decanter and tossed it back in one swallow. Then he moved to the desk and picked up the cordless phone that sat on the surface. They listened as he made a business call.

Rafe thought it would never end, Sara was still pressed against him, and his nostrils were filled with the honey-ginger scent of her shampoo, and an underlying fragrance that was hers alone. She was soft and supple against him, and he felt his body hardening in response.

He knew the precise instant that she became aware of his arousal, when her breath hitched unevenly and she stilled in his arms. Then slowly, she leaned forward and pressed her lips against his throat. Rafe swallowed hard.

In the office, he heard Edwin finish his phone call and hang up the phone. There was silence for a long moment until finally, with a soft oath, Edwin left the room. The door closed behind him with a decisive click, yet Rafe didn't release Sara.

"We should go," she murmured against his throat. "Before we get caught."

"Mmm. We should." But he couldn't resist lowering his head and covering her mouth with his own, savoring her immediate response. His hands slid to where her warm skin was exposed by the strapless cocktail gown. He traced his fingers along the gentle slope of her shoulders, and she made a soft sound of encouragement.

He wanted to press her back against the closet wall, push her skirt up and bury himself in her welcoming heat. He wanted to keep her in the protective circle of his arms and never let her out of his sight. Hell, he just wanted to keep her.

She pulled away first, her breath fanning warmly against his face. "We need to leave before someone finds us," she whispered.

She was right. They'd been lucky that Edwin hadn't discovered them, but their luck might not hold out. Reluctantly, he released her.

"You're right. Let's get the hell out of here."

SARA'S HEART BEAT FAST, both from the fear of being discovered and from Rafe's kisses. She followed him swiftly through the office and into the adjacent sitting room, closing the office door carefully. Keeping her behind him, Rafe entered the main hallway and nearly collided with a woman.

"Mrs. Zachary," he said smoothly, stepping back. "Excuse us—we were looking for the powder room."

Diane Zachary's startled gaze flew from Rafe to Sara and then to the closed door of her husband's office. "The bathrooms are located along the main corridor, on the left," she said coolly. Her gaze lingered on Sara. "Ms. Sinclair, wasn't it?"

"Yes, that's right. From *American Man* magazine." Sara strove for a calm tone as she extended her hand to the other woman, but Diane didn't take it. Instead, her gaze dropped to the abrasion that extended from Sara's elbow to her forearm.

"That's a nasty scrape you have there."

Sara withdrew her hand and tucked it behind her, casting a quick glance at Rafe. His expression was inscrutable. "Oh, that," she said lightly. "It's nothing, really. I fell the other night."

"Hmm." Diane gave her a patently false smile. "You should be more careful when you're crossing the street. Now, if you'll excuse me, I'm looking for my husband."

But as she tried to step past them into the sitting room, Rafe caught her by the arm. She narrowed her eyes at him and opened her mouth to speak, but he didn't give her a chance.

"I don't believe Ms. Sinclair mentioned anything about crossing a street," he said, his voice deceptively soft. "How would you know that information? Were you, by any chance, driving through Chinatown last night in a Lincoln Town Car?"

They stared at each other for a long moment, before

Diane snatched her arm free. "Keep your hands off me. Who do you think you are?" she hissed.

"I'm the man who's been trying to keep Ms. Sinclair alive for the past five days, despite your attempts to prevent that."

Diane gasped, but Sara didn't miss the quick fear that leapt into her eyes. "What are you suggesting? I don't know Ms. Sinclair. I've never even met her before tonight."

"But you knew that she'd discovered your husband's involvement with a certain club, didn't you? And knowing that she's a writer for *American Man* magazine, you'd stop at nothing to prevent her from making his association with the club public knowledge. Isn't that right?"

A group of elegantly dressed women were making their way down the corridor toward them, and with a small noise of frustration, Diane indicated that Rafe and Sara should precede her into her husband's office. Only when the door was closed behind them did she speak again.

"I never intended to hurt Ms. Sinclair," she said, tipping her chin up and fixing Sara with an icy glare. "I only meant to scare you enough that you'd think twice about publicizing my husband's behavior."

"And which behavior would that be?" Sara asked. "The sexual fantasies he purchases through the Glass Slipper Club, or his affair with Lauren Black?"

Diane gave Sara a frigid smile. "Don't you know? They're one and the same."

Rafe frowned. "What are you talking about?"

Diane gave him a look of disdain. "For all your intelligence contacts, Sergeant, you really don't know, do you? Lauren Black may very well work as an editor for *American Man* magazine, but she moonlights for the Glass Slipper Club under the name Lisette."

Lisette. Sara recalled seeing the name on the client list. Judging by the frequency with which the name had appeared, Lisette was one of the more popular call girls in the club. But *Lauren?* Smart, acerbic, get-the-job-done Lauren?

"That's impossible," Sara protested. "I know Lauren, and she would never demean herself by doing something like that."

Diane gave a bitter laugh. "Trust me, dear. I've had detectives following my husband now for months and I have explicit photos of Edwin with that woman." She passed a hand over her eyes. "I even confronted him with the proof that I know about his activities, but the man is ruled by his dick. He truly can't help himself."

Sara moved closer to Rafe's protective bulk. "Were those your detectives who responded to the break-in at my apartment?"

"Dear, those were my detectives who *performed* the break-in at your apartment. I pay Anderson and Michaels very well for their services. And now I know that you have a memory stick that contains certain information. What is it? A list of clients?"

"You'll never know," Sara said hotly.

"I want that client list, Ms. Sinclair." Diane's face twisted and her voice was fierce. "I've worked as hard as any whore to get where I am today. I knew Edwin was a womanizer when I married him, but I also knew he had what it took to go all the way to the top. I've put up with his philandering ways for years, cleaning up his messes and doing it with a smile." She was almost spitting in her fury. "I've given away millions of dollars in charity to ensure he has the connections he needs for a presidential campaign, and I'm not about to let you ruin it by publicizing his connection with the Glass Slipper Club. I can destroy you with a snap of my fingers, Ms. Sinclair, do you understand that?"

Rafe stepped in front of Sara. "You're not going to do anything, Mrs. Zachary. That list is somewhere safe, where you'll never get your hands on it. If you want it to remain a secret, you'll ensure that nothing happens to Ms. Sinclair."

Diane turned her furious gaze to Rafe, sweeping him with a disdainful look. "Who do you think you are? I've spent years pandering to the Washington elite, and there isn't anyone who doesn't owe me a favor. With one call to the Pentagon, I could have your stripes."

Anxiety stabbed at Sara. She'd never heard anyone so callously threaten to ruin a man's career as Diane had just done. And Sara had no doubt that she could do it.

But instead of looking upset, Rafe gave Diane a slow, predatory smile. Even in his formal evening wear, he looked dangerous. "Go ahead," he purred. "But after you make that call, be sure to pick up a copy of the *Washington Post*. And the *Washington Times* and the *Express*, because I think you'll be interested in the headlines. Do I make myself clear?"

"You bastard," Diana hissed. "I will not be made the butt of jokes amongst the political pundits, nor will I be an object of pity for the Washington elite. If this information becomes public knowledge, I won't be one of those women who stands by her husband with a look of long-suffering tolerance while he apologizes to the

American public for his transgressions. I can't let you publish that list."

Rafe moved quickly, pushing Diane back against the door of the office with his hands on her shoulders and his face scant inches from hers. His expression was ruthless.

"If anything—*anything*—happens to Sara, I'll personally ensure that a copy of that client list is delivered to the senior editor of every daily newspaper in Washington. And then I'll come after you." Diane's cool façade cracked and she stared at Rafe with undisguised fear in her eyes. "So I'd say it's in your best interest to keep her alive and healthy."

He stepped back, dropping his hands from the woman's shoulders as if he found the act of touching her personally distasteful.

"It's men like you who make this world a dangerous place to live," Diane said in a low, tight voice.

"That's where you're wrong," he snarled softly. "It's people like you, who believe the rules don't apply, who make this world a dangerous place." He extended a hand to Sara. "But you're right about one thing. I am a dangerous man. I'd remember that, if I were you."

RAFE HANDED SARA INTO the limousine before he climbed in to sit on the padded seat across from her. Guests were still arriving at the Zachary residence as they pulled away, but Sara was grateful to be leaving.

"What a horrible woman," she exclaimed. "Maybe we should just blow the entire story wide open and watch her go to prison for what she tried to do."

Leaning forward, Rafe pressed a button and the privacy screen slid smoothly into place behind the driver.

"I think Diane Zachary is already in a prison of sorts," he said quietly, "just one of her own making. She knows that if anything happens to you, she'll lose everything. As for Edwin, I guarantee he won't run for President. He'll end up destroying his own career. That's good enough for me. Are you okay?"

Sara nodded and then slanted him a questioning look. "Where is the memory stick?"

Rafe laughed softly. "I have no idea. I sent it to a friend in North Carolina and told him to put it somewhere safe. I'm guessing it's stored in a weapons bunker at Fort Bragg, protected by concertina wire and reinforced doors, not to mention the U.S. Army."

Sara frowned. "Do you believe what she said about Lauren being one of the call girls?"

Rafe shrugged. "After what I've seen these past few days, I'm inclined to believe just about anything."

"Do you think Lauren was involved in any of what happened? I mean, she invited me to the Singapore Bistro that night. Maybe she knew about the client list."

"I don't think so. But maybe you should talk to her."

"You're right," she said, pulling her cell phone out of her small evening bag. "It's bad enough that she had an affair with Edwin Zachary! No wonder she didn't want to go to the book-signing. But I can't believe she's involved in the Glass Slipper Club. I won't believe it until I hear it from her."

She punched in the number and waited until Lauren answered. "How's the book-signing?" the editor asked without preamble. "Did you get a quote from Edwin Zachary?"

Sara glanced at Rafe. "Unfortunately, no. But I did get one from Diane Zachary."

"Oh. Well, let's hear it. Did she have anything interesting to say?"

"I think so. She said you moonlight for the Glass Slipper Club under the name Lisette." She waited expectantly for an outraged protest, but there was only silence. "Lauren, we saw photos of you and Edwin Zachary together. Do you deny it?"

"Oh, what's the point?" Lauren asked, exasperated. "Fine. Yes, I work part-time for the club. Are you happy now?"

Sara couldn't suppress the disappointment and dismay she felt. "Why, Lauren? You're a senior editor at *American Man* magazine. You're well respected in the industry and it's not as if you need the money. Please tell me why you'd be involved in something like that, because it just doesn't make any sense to me."

"What? You think only drug addicts or desperate women become call girls?" Lauren asked, her voice filled with derision. "Let me tell you something, sweetie. Most of the women who work for the Glass Slipper Club are highly educated, attractive women. They're lawyers and college professors and reputable businesswomen."

"So why do it?" Sara asked. "You're intelligent and attractive—you could have any man you want."

Lauren laughed. "I don't want a man in my life, darling, just in my bed. I like sex. Hell, I love sex without any of the messy complications that come with a committed relationship. And Washington is a very expensive place to live. Plus, I get to screw some seriously powerful men. You wouldn't believe the pillow talks I've had."

Sara's gaze flew to Rafe's. He watched her intently.

"Is that how you found out about Rafe Delgado's involvement with the rescue of the aid workers? Through one of your clients?"

"That was an unexpected perk," Lauren admitted. "I've actually gotten the inside scoop on several great stories as a result of my club connections. You know, with a face and body like yours, you could make a bundle in this particular line of work. Think of it as a way to make your most secret fantasies come true."

"The Glass Slipper Club is done, Lauren. Even if I hadn't discovered what was going on, the Feds were getting ready to pull the plug on the whole operation. Juliet's likely left the country and the club has closed its doors." Sara let her gaze slide over Rafe as he eased a finger inside his collar and loosened his bow tie. "Besides, there are other ways to fulfill your fantasies without selling your soul."

"So does this mean I'm not getting my story about the rescue?" Lauren asked.

"I'll get you a story," Sara promised. "Just not the one you were looking for."

She closed her cell phone and considered Rafe. He leaned back against the luxurious seat, looking every inch a dark, sexy playboy in his disheveled tuxedo.

"I heard most of that," he admitted.

Sara sighed. "I still can't quite believe it. I'll give her one last story, but then I'm done with the magazine."

Rafe frowned. "Are you sure? What will you do?"

Sara smiled and leaned forward, placing her hands on his strong thighs. "Oh, I have a few ideas." She slid her hands higher, closing the small distance between them. Climbing onto the seat, she scooted forward until her knees bracketed his legs and she could kneel upright and thread her fingers into his hair.

Rafe smiled lazily into her eyes. "I'm listening."

"I was just thinking that you could help me fulfill another one of my fantasies."

"I think we may already have explored this one," he said huskily.

"Mmm. But not in a limousine."

His eyes darkened and his hands slid under the hem of her dress, sliding up to smooth over her buttocks. "You're wearing a thong," he groaned. "I didn't know you even owned a thong."

She smiled and lowered her mouth to his, her breathing quickening as he pushed the flimsy material to one side. "A girl has to have a few secrets. And this is a really great fantasy, but it's not the fantasy I was referring to."

"No?"

"Nope. You're my fantasy," she breathed. "Being with you is my fantasy. Loving you is my fantasy."

Rafe looked at her, his expression soft and sexy. "That's an easy one to fulfill," he rasped, "because you're my fantasy, too."

Epilogue

Two months later

IT WAS ALMOST MIDNIGHT. Sara didn't know how long she'd been curled up on her sofa, staring dreamily at the multicolored lights on her small Christmas tree. But she knew if she didn't get to bed soon, she'd regret it in the morning. Tomorrow was a big day, and she needed all the sleep she could get. Standing up, she stretched and was about to pad across her small apartment to turn off the lights when someone knocked softly on her apartment door, causing her to jump.

"Who's there?" she called.

"It's me," came the deep response.

With her heart leaping in her chest, Sara unbolted the door and flung it wide, drinking in the sight of the man who stood in the hallway. He'd only been gone a month, but it felt like much longer. He'd spent the past four weeks training in North Carolina, and although they had talked to each other nearly every day, Sara had missed him.

"Rafe." He wore his Marine Corps dress blues and carried a duffel bag in one hand. "What are you doing

here? I wasn't expecting you until tomorrow." Her hand flew self-consciously to her hair, and then to her pajama top. "If I'd known you were coming, I would have worn something...hot."

With a soft laugh, Rafe stepped into her apartment and dropped his duffel onto the floor before he drew her into his arms. His uniform still carried the chill of outdoors and Sara shivered as she wreathed her arms around his neck.

"You *do* look hot. And I didn't want to wait until tomorrow to see you. To be with you."

"Why didn't you call me?" she asked, pressing kisses against his jaw, his neck and his lips. "I would have come to the airport to get you."

"I didn't call because I wanted to find you exactly like this," he growled, hauling her close and capturing her mouth in a searing kiss. "Warm and soft and welcoming."

"Mmm. I was just going to bed."

"Then my timing is perfect."

Before Sara could protest, he lifted her in his arms. She gave a startled laugh of surprise and clutched him around his shoulders, deciding she didn't really need to sleep, after all. Rafe strode toward her bedroom, then paused. Sara twisted in his arms to see what he was looking at and her gaze fell on the most recent issue of *American Man* magazine. On the cover was a picture of Corporal Shay Riordan surrounded by other injured soldiers. Behind them was the Walter Reed hospital. The caption beside the photo read, True Blue American Heroes.

Sara had written a story that focused on Shay's heroism and the Semper Fi Fund's efforts to support the men and women recuperating at the hospital. She had emphasized the need for the public to do the same as a way to thank the soldiers who had given so much. Already, donations to the Fund were pouring in, and the hospital had reported a surge in visitors, including celebrities and people who wanted to help.

"Did I thank you yet for doing the story on the Semper Fi Fund?" he asked. "And not on the rescue mission in Pakistan?"

"I think so," she said, "but it definitely bears repeating. Everyone is entitled to keep a secret or two. And yours are safe with me."

Rafe carried her into the bedroom and laid her down on the bed, following closely with the length of his body against hers. "I have a whole new appreciation for the benefits of the media," he murmured, dipping his head to kiss the soft swell of her breast above her camisole top. "Why didn't you tell me today was your last at the magazine?"

Sara rolled her head on the covers and looked at him with amusement. "Because I knew you probably already knew. And I was right. When did you find out?"

Rafe kicked his shoes off and propped himself on one elbow as he smoothed his hand over her body. "Just last week. So what will you do now?"

Sara rolled toward him, hitching a thigh across his hips and drawing his head down for a deep kiss. "I was offered a job as a staff reporter for the *Washington Post*, courtesy of Diane Zachary. And that was *after* her husband was caught in a compromising situation with a White House intern. He has a press conference scheduled later this week to publicly apologize, and to formally withdraw his bid for the Presidency."

Rafe gave a huff of laughter. "No shit. I wonder if Diane will be at his side when he makes the announcement. Are you going to take the job?"

"Absolutely not. I think it's clear I'm not cut out to be an investigative reporter. I found a job writing for a women's magazine, instead. I really like the editor and I think it's going to be a good match."

"Congratulations. What did Lauren have to say?"

"She gave me a good recommendation, and said that if I ever want my old job back, she'd hire me in a heartbeat."

Rafe laughed softly and pressed a kiss against her bare shoulder. "I have some news that I was going to save until tomorrow, but since we're sharing secrets, I may as well tell you now."

Sara waited expectantly, unable to tell from his expression if she was going to welcome the news or not.

"I've accepted an assignment as a military strategist at the Pentagon. I report for duty right after the holidays."

"Rafe." Sara stared at him, too overcome to say anything else, but the implications weren't lost on her. He wouldn't return to Afghanistan or Pakistan. His life would no longer be in danger. He wouldn't have to leave her again. She buried her face against his shoulder, her fingers curling into the fabric of his uniform.

"Hey," he said gently, tipping her face up. "Are you crying? I thought you'd be happy."

"I am," she assured him, swiping at her damp cheeks. "I can't tell you how happy that makes me. I don't have to worry about your safety anymore."

"Better yet, I'll be right here with you, which means I won't need to worry about your safety anymore, either."

Sara wound her arms around his neck and pressed herself closer. "I'm so happy. You see, I may need you around to help me fulfill my remaining fantasies."

Rafe groaned and hauled her closer. "Sweetheart, I am definitely the man for the job. Let me show you..."

It turned out, Sara thought happily, that all of the best things happened after midnight.

* * * * *

COMING NEXT MONTH

Available October 25, 2011

#645 THE SURVIVOR
Men Out of Uniform
Rhonda Nelson

#646 MODEL MARINE
Uniformly Hot!
Candace Havens

#647 THE MIGHTY QUINNS: DANNY
The Mighty Quinns
Kate Hoffmann

#648 INTOXICATING
Lori Wilde

#649 ROPED IN
The Wrong Bed
Crystal Green

#650 ROYALLY CLAIMED
A Real Prince
Marie Donovan

HBCNM1011

Harlequin® Special Edition® is thrilled to present a new installment in USA TODAY *bestselling author RaeAnne Thayne's reader-favorite miniseries,* THE COWBOYS OF COLD CREEK.

Join the excitement as we meet the Bowmans—four siblings who lost their parents but keep family ties alive in Pine Gulch. First up is Trace. Only two things get under this rugged lawman's skin: beautiful women and secrets. And in Rebecca Parsons, he finds both!

Read on for a sneak peek of CHRISTMAS IN COLD CREEK. Available November 2011 from Harlequin® Special Edition®.

On impulse, he unfolded himself from the bar stool. "Need a hand?"

"Thank you! I..." She lifted her gaze from the floor to his jeans and then raised her eyes. When she identified him her hazel eyes turned from grateful to unfriendly and cold, as if he'd somehow thrown the broken glasses at her head.

He also thought he saw a glimmer of panic in those interesting depths, which instantly stirred his curiosity like cream swirling through coffee.

"I've got it, Officer. Thank you." Her voice was several degrees colder than the whirl of sleet outside the windows.

Despite her protests, he knelt down beside her and began to pick up shards of broken glass. "No problem. Those trays can be slippery."

This close, he picked up the scent of her, something fresh and flowery that made him think of a mountain meadow on a July afternoon. She had a soft, lush mouth and for one brief, insane moment, he wanted to push aside that stray lock of hair slipping from her ponytail and taste her. Apparently he needed to spend a lot less time working and a great deal *more* time recreating with the opposite sex if he could have sudden random fantasies about a woman he wasn't even inclined to like, pretty or not.

"I'm Trace Bowman. You must be new in town."

She didn't answer immediately and he could almost see the wheels turning in her head. Why the hesitancy? And why that little hint of unease he could see clouding the edge of her gaze? His presence was obviously making her uncomfortable and Trace couldn't help wondering why.

"Yes. We've been here a few weeks."

"Well, I'm just up the road about four lots, in the white house with the cedar shake roof, if you or your daughter need anything." He smiled at her as he picked up the last shard of glass and set it on her tray.

Definitely a story there, he thought as she hurried away. He just might need to dig a little into her background to find out why someone with fine clothes and nice jewelry, and who so obviously didn't have experience as a waitress, would be here slinging hash at The Gulch. Was she running away from someone? A bad marriage?

So…Rebecca Parsons. Not Becky. An intriguing woman. It had been a long time since one of those had crossed his path here in Pine Gulch.

Trace won't rest until he finds out Rebecca's secret, but will he still have that same attraction to her once he does?
Find out in CHRISTMAS IN COLD CREEK.
Available November 2011 from Harlequin® Special Edition®.

HSEEXP1111